THE LANDLORD

C.V. HUNT
ANDERSEN PRUNTY

GRINDHOUSE
PRESS

Grindhouse Press #113
ISBN-13: 978-1-957504-27-8

You should be reading books written by Bentley Little.

1

ROBIN WAS STRETCHED OUT ON the recliner, doomscrolling through her phone. The late afternoon sun blasted through the west-facing windows of the living room apartment, warming her bare legs. She grew impatient with the quality of the videos she'd been watching the last half hour and decided to check her latest sales on Bee's Knees, a fetish site for knee enthusiasts. Her newest photos had only garnered three sales since Wednesday's photo session. Disappointed, she set her phone on the armrest, looked at her knees, and noticed the sunlight shining on them was perfect. It was the golden hour. The ideal time for photos. She knew she shouldn't be working on a Saturday but Marcus was working and it would only take a minute.

She set the recliner upright, grabbed the plant stand housing the spider plant, and pulled the stand to position it between her legs. She snapped a couple of photos with her phone of her knees on either side of the plant. She was reviewing and editing the photos when there was a knock on the apartment door, followed by a *swish* sound.

Robin headed toward the door and spotted a paper on the floor in front of it. She picked it up and read it as she walked toward the bedroom.

Saturday was normally a lazy day for Marcus and Robin since they both worked from home. They'd agreed when Robin moved in they wouldn't work on the weekends. Having the weekends off allowed them to nurture their fledgling relationship. They'd met in an online forum for entrepreneurs eight months ago and things quickly snowballed. Robin had moved in with Marcus just three months prior. But things were financially tight for the new couple and that was why Marcus was in the bedroom filling a few orders for his online endeavor, Open Air—an artisanal air capturing business. Throughout the week Marcus would drive to parks or wooded areas and capture jars of the fresh air and sell them online.

A corner of their bedroom acted as an office for Marcus since the apartment was only a one-bedroom. He was printing out the last shipping label when Robin walked in holding a paper, staring at the text on it.

Robin sighed. "They're raising the rent."

"You've got to be kidding me," Marcus said. "How much is it this time?"

"Two hundred dollars a month."

"What!? That's ridiculous. It was only twenty dollars last year."

"I don't think I can come up with any more money each month through Bee's Knees. And I really don't want to go back to selling my used underwear."

Marcus placed the last order in a tote to take to the post office on Monday. "No," he said. "You don't have to go back to doing that if you don't want to. I've had enough. We'll find a new place." He approached Robin, took the paper from her hands, crumpled it, and tossed it in the waste basket. He wrapped his arms around her. "It only seems fitting, since we're starting a new life together, to start it in a new place."

Robin bit her lip. "The move *here* wiped out my bank account. I don't know if I can help much with moving expenses."

"Don't worry. I have a little in my savings. Probably just enough for the deposit and first month. Besides, I should get the deposit back for this place."

"Thank you. I'll pay it back somehow. I don't want you to feel like I'm not pulling my weight."

2

Marcus smiled at her. "Oh, I'm sure we can work something out." He kissed her and slid his hands down her back and grabbed her ass.

"Mmmm. Maybe we can take it out in trade?"

The couple fell onto the bed and made love, forgetting about the stress of moving for a little while.

Later that evening they sat silently in the living room. Robin scrolled through photos of rentals near the apartment they currently rented. Marcus did the same on his laptop.

"There's just nothing available," Robin said.

"And what is available is more expensive than what we're gonna be paying with the rent increase," Marcus said.

"Maybe we should look somewhere else."

"Like where?"

Robin shrugged. "What about something outside of the city?"

"The suburbs?" Marcus made a disgusted face.

"No, like out in the country. Some place quiet."

"I don't know."

They both continued to search their devices for an answer.

Robin opened the map app on her phone and scrolled to the edge of the city, zooming in and out, looking for town names. She spotted a town named Little Falls. From the view of the map, it looked like a small town with the necessities: post office, gas station, grocery store. It also appeared to have a few restaurants and bars. There was even a Dollar General on the edge of town, the only chain store within twenty miles. She opened the internet app and typed "Little Falls classifieds" and was redirected to the town's newspaper site, which looked like it was designed in the late '90s. Robin scrolled until she found the rentals.

"Whoa," she said.

Marcus didn't look up from his laptop. "Find something?"

"Maybe." She read the ad to him. "One bedroom house with bonus room. Furnished. Available June first."

He looked at her. "That's a week from today. What's the rent?"

"Says eight hundred. Seems pretty cheap."

"Yeah, but there's probably a reason. Where's it located."

"In Little Falls. Not too far from the city. It says to text Peter Slager and there's a number. It can't hurt to look at it. If it's still available." She watched him think it over.

"Go ahead and text them. For eight hundred it's either already taken or there's something seriously wrong with it."

THE LANDLORD

Robin checked the time to make sure it wasn't too late and texted the number. After she sent the text she said, "Probably won't hear back until tomorrow."

Her phone chimed. They both looked at it. She checked the message and said, "Or I'll hear back from him immediately."

"What does it say?"

She laughed. "Wanna go look at it tomorrow afternoon?"

"There's definitely something wrong with it."

Robin typed away on her phone. "One o'clock it is."

2

ASIDE FROM ITS SIZE, THE most curious thing about the house was the man standing on the roof. The weather had broken about five minutes outside of Little Falls, rain hammering down while thunder rumbled and lightning flashed in the distance. The man, presumably the landlord, was soaked. He spotted them waiting in their car.

"Christ, the roof probably leaks," Marcus muttered, already sounding defeated.

Robin rolled down the passenger-side window. Rain immediately bounced off the window edge and began soaking her.

"Are you here to look at the house!" the man shouted.

"Yeah!" Robin shouted back.

"Go on in. I'll be down in a second."

Robin put her window back up. She wiped the rain off her arms and onto the floor mat of the car, as if it mattered once she was outside.

"Ready to run for it?" she said.

"I'll walk briskly," Marcus returned, his disdain of physical activity a long-held passion.

From the road, they were maybe only twenty-five steps from the house. They both unlatched their doors and paused.

"And … go!" Robin blurted.

They got out of the car, hopped an old railroad beam separating the yard from the parking space, and sloshed across the cobblestone walkway until they stood in front of the screen door that looked like it had been pulled out of the trash sometime in the mid-'80s.

"Don't forget to take off your shoes!" the landlord practically howled from the roof.

Marcus raised his eyebrows, widened his eyes, and said, "Sounds serious," before opening the screen door, standing just inside, and pulling off his weird barefoot shoes.

For the next minute or so, they stood painfully close on a towel just inside the door, each of them holding their dripping shoes in their hands.

"I guess we'll just put these right here." Robin leaned over and placed her shoes on the towel next to a pair of ratty, knock-off Birkenstocks presumably owned by the landlord.

Marcus let his drop.

They were both looking around the tiny house, seemingly speechless. There were two gamer chairs in what would be considered the living room, along with a rickety-looking TV stand with an older TV, an end table, a floor lamp, and bookshelves built into the wall, all of which filled the space with little room to walk around. A two-person dinette was crammed between the living room and the kitchenette. There even appeared to be a few dirty dishes in the sink. Robin knew the place came furnished but it downright appeared like someone still lived there. Marcus and Robin were taking in the situation, saying nothing to one another, until they were interrupted by the landlord.

Marcus was just getting ready to ask Robin to remind her what the guy's name was again.

The landlord shook off before entering the house and wiping his bare feet with the towel all the shoes were resting on. His thinning blond hair dripped into his bulgy blue eyes. He was about a decade older than either of them and struck Robin as a cross between Sting and Michael Stipe.

"You must be Robin." He held out his hand.

"I am." She shook his still moist hand. "Nice to meet you, Peter.

This is my partner, Marcus."

Peter turned to Marcus and they shook hands. "I used to work with a guy named Marcus."

Marcus didn't know how to respond so he just said, "It's a name."

"Okay," Peter said. "I guess you're here to see the house. This should be quick. It's a small house, only 400 square feet. Twenty by twenty. I was up on the roof because I've been thinking about installing a lightning rod and I wanted to make sure it was stable enough to support it. I want it to reach above the trees so it's the highest thing in the yard. That way you don't have to worry about lightning striking one of the trees and falling on it. When I lived here, I kept my bed— well, mattress—right under the roof."

Robin kept her bright-eyed, smiling face held tight but, already, she could tell this guy was kind of a lot.

"We're just glad the roof wasn't leaking," Marcus said. Robin initially thought it was a challenge to Peter's masculinity until she reminded herself that Marcus didn't have much of that and was probably saying whatever because he was nervous.

"Oh no, this house is tight, well put-together. I built a house on the outskirts of town and completely rebuilt this one using spare materials. Sorry to be a psycho about the shoes, but I just installed the floor and I'm pretty proud of it."

The floor was a hodge-podge of mismatched boards, some of them real wood and some of them engineered to look like wood. Robin thought he should have hastened its destruction as an excuse to replace it.

As he showed them around the house, Robin wasn't sure anything made sense even after his explanations. What would serve as the living room and dining/kitchen area occupied half the house closest to the road. They still collectively stood in the three-by-three area comprising the world's smallest foyer. He pointed out the most obvious thing in the space, a spiraling wooden staircase that looked like it was carved from a random pile of wood and occupied roughly a quarter of the living area.

"Woodworking is one of my hobbies. This is all native wood I dragged out of the reserve. Same as the bookcases." He motioned to the massive bookcases built into the living area. They were stained dark and lent an oppressive, foreboding atmosphere to that section of the house.

He continued. "Full-size washer and dryer there under the

staircase."

Robin immediately imagined hitting her head … a lot.

He pointed out the small refrigerator and two-burner gas stove. "Let's look at the rest of the house," he said.

He took four or so steps from the front door, Robin and Marcus following, before they all stood in a room far smaller than Robin's childhood bedroom. A desk was pushed up against the wall under one of the windows. A clothes rack, loaded with clothes, and a dresser also occupied the room. Robin wasn't sure what the situation was with the clothes and assumed the previous tenants either left them behind or were possibly still living there.

"Like I said, I slept upstairs but this would make a good guest bedroom or an office or something. I hope you noticed the windows throughout the house. It helps make it feel a little bigger, especially in the summer. I like having everything open and letting the outside in."

"We're in an apartment now, so any access to the outdoors is great," Marcus said.

They all shifted around so they could follow Peter out of the room. He led them back through the living area, dining area, and down a short, narrow hallway.

"Here's the bathroom," Peter said. "It's small but it has a full-size sink and tub."

Robin immersed herself in the bathroom while Marcus leaned against the frame and noticed the odd smell coming from it. It wasn't necessarily a waste smell, just dank … or something. A towel was draped over the shower curtain rod and could have been a source of the smell but Marcus didn't think so.

"This'll work," Robin said, noting that if they ended up taking the place they'd have to warn their larger-sized friends and family in the gentlest way possible.

"Yeah," Peter said. "It's small enough you can brush your teeth while sitting on the toilet."

Efficient, Robin thought. *No wasted space.* Then she thought about that staircase. *Lots of wasted space, unfortunately.*

The landlord pointed toward the window of the door leading to the backyard. "I built a small shed in the backyard to store your lawnmower in. You'll be responsible for the upkeep of the yard. The previous tenant left their equipment you can use." Peter clapped his hands and said, "Ready to take a look upstairs?"

They followed him back down the hall into the living area.

"You have to duck so you don't hit your head." He proceeded to climb the disproportionately large staircase like a scrabbling primate. Robin and Marcus followed.

At the top of the stairs, he sat down in a doorway about three feet high, grabbed a hook light from the floor and turned it on. Robin expected him to start telling a spooky story or singing Roy Orbison's "In Dreams."

"I mostly slept on the floor, but you can probably get a queen mattress up here."

"That's what we have," Robin said.

"How long have you been married?"

"Oh," Robin said. "We've been together a little under a year. Not married yet. But we've both been there before." She didn't want to tell him they'd only known each other eight months, most of that online, assuming he may see them as risky renters.

"I totally get it," Peter said. "I went through a rough divorce about a decade ago. I really thought Daniel was the love of my life. But … didn't work out. We're still good friends though. Actually, he lives across the alley. He probably thought it was weird when I moved out and took the place right behind him but … well, it's a pricey little town and it was the only thing available in my budget."

That's not just weird, it's psychotic, Robin thought, saying, "It's nice that you still have him in your life though."

"He's one of the good ones." A faraway look came over Peter's eyes before he scooted back into the darkened room behind him, never uncrossing his legs. "This room's really too small to use as anything other than storage, although I guess a pretty small person could sleep in here. I don't mind if you paint some of the walls in the house, but I ask that you not touch these."

Marcus and Robin looked around in the meager light of the hook lamp. The walls were covered in artwork.

"Daniel did this. He's quite the artist."

Robin begged to differ. She was sure Marcus did too. Luckily he was the one to step up to the plate this time. "Yeah. This is really good. Colorful. Psychedelic."

Peter laughed. "I think we were on mushrooms at the time."

"Perfect vibe," Marcus said.

Peter asked them all the usual questions—where they lived, worked, how long they were looking to rent for, how many cars or pets they had—and Robin and Marcus struggled to work in questions about the house. Robin managed to ask about the clothes in the downstairs bedroom.

"Everything stays," the landlord said. "The previous renter moved to another country. Couldn't take much with him. You're welcome to keep what you need. Just set the rest at the curb. The people of Little Falls are pretty resourceful. Someone will need it or use it."

By the time they walked out to their car nearly an hour later, it felt like they'd been at the bar with an old, very energetic friend.

Peter told them he had a few more showings later and said he'd make a decision and get back with them, if they wanted it.

They shut their car doors and breathed matching sighs of ... what? Confusion?

"We're totally taking it, right?" Marcus said.

Robin smiled. "It's too ridiculous to say no to."

"We probably won't get it."

When they got home, Robin texted Peter to tell him they were extremely interested in the house.

A few days later, he told them it was all theirs.

They had a celebratory dinner and immediately began packing.

3

"THIS IS ABSURD, RIGHT? ARE we out of our fucking minds?" Robin grabbed a stack of LPs from the dolly she'd borrowed from the laundry area. She chucked them into one of the three overflowing dumpsters behind the apartment building and laughed when she heard them break.

Marcus had spent the entire day playing as many records as he could, sorting out anything that skipped. He grabbed a handful of the LPs and looked at them forlornly before tossing them into the nearly overflowing dumpster. "We don't have too many options. We're moving from seven hundred square feet to four hundred square feet. We can't take it all with us. Besides, the less we have, the less we have to move."

"Yeah, moving is no fun. And I'm doing it twice in three months. What are we gonna do about the furniture?"

"I don't know. I guess wheel it down here and set it beside the dumpster. The only thing we're taking with us is the mattress for the loft and a couple of the bookshelves for the office, or um,"—he made

11

quotations with his fingers—"'the bonus room.'"

"It feels like I'm throwing my life away." Robin tossed the last of the records into the dumpster. "All this stuff we own. What does it really matter? It's just stuff."

"Whatever we have to tell ourselves to not have an existential crisis about throwing away years of memories and thousands of dollars." Marcus pushed the dolly toward the building for another round of material things they would no longer have room for when they moved tomorrow.

Once they were on the elevator, Robin's phone chimed with an incoming message. She checked the message. "Peter texted to say he emailed the lease to me. We need to sign it and get it back to him ASAP."

"I was wondering if he was ever gonna send it. Nothing like waiting until the last minute. I hope this isn't a sign that he's a flaky landlord."

Robin was focused on the lease, looking for any loopholes. "I think we can sign it from my phone." She continued to read the document to herself. She hoped it wasn't a terrible decision they'd be bound to for one year.

The elevator chimed and the door opened to their floor. They were both assaulted with the reek of the trash chute.

"Oh god," Robin said. "I'll be glad when I don't have to smell that anymore."

"Me too. Fucking gag-inducing."

Marcus began stacking more stuff onto the dolly once they were back inside the apartment. Robin was still reading the lease, her face twisting into a confused mask.

Marcus noticed Robin's expression and asked, "What's wrong?"

"I don— Nothing, I think. The lease reads a little weird is all." She laughed.

"Oh no. Weird how?"

Without looking up from her phone she said, "Just … it's apparent he wrote this himself. There are a lot of typos. There's a clause about dogs. Cats are okay but no dogs. Weird, but okay, I'm not a dog fan either. And it's very specific about how to clean the house and which cleaners can be used. There's also a section that says you can't run a business out of the house." She looked at Marcus, concerned. "Does that mean we can't live there? We both work from home."

"I think he probably means you can't use the house as a business. We're not doing that. Our business is online. We don't have customers coming to the house. Besides, he asked what we did and we told him we work from home."

Robin made an uncertain sound. "We didn't tell him we ran our own businesses. He might've assumed we worked remote."

Marcus said, "It's better to do it and ask for forgiveness later. I'm sure it won't be a problem."

"I hope so." Robin fidgeted with her phone and handed it to Marcus. "You can use your finger to sign."

Marcus signed the lease and handed the phone back to Robin. She signed it and typed out a quick message before emailing the lease back to Peter.

"Does it seem weird that he never asked for paystubs? Or any proof of income?" Marcus said. "He didn't even bother to ask to look at our driver's licenses or run a background check on either of us."

Robin shrugged. "Small town? Maybe he's a trusting guy. Might be the reason for some of the weird clauses in the lease. He might've gotten screwed over by a previous tenant."

"Maybe. Now …" Marcus grabbed the handle of the dolly. "Let the purge continue."

~

They took a dinner break around five to order some burritos from a local Mexican place. While they were eating, Marcus's brother, Roger, showed up to help.

Roger carried a jug of something with him. He greeted Robin and Marcus before putting the jug on their counter.

"What's that?" Marcus asked.

"Good news," Roger said. "I got hired at the Little Falls Brewery. This is a growler of their finest."

"Awesome," Marcus said. "How'd you score that?"

"I was on a beer forum talking to this guy named Jeremiah who happens to work there. He put in a good word for me. You guys still need help?"

"Absolutely. I don't know how we managed to fit so much shit in a 700-square-foot space. We could probably use a second car too." Marcus finished his burrito and crumpled the foil.

"I didn't think I'd regret getting rid of my car so soon," Robin said. "Just seems easier and cheaper to share a car."

"You still have any glasses around?" Roger asked.

"Same place as always," Marcus said. "I don't know how we're going to pack them. We're almost out of boxes."

Roger set three pint glasses down and filled them with the golden beer. He put the growler in the refrigerator. "Let's toast to the new place," he said.

They all clinked glasses and took sips.

"That's good," Robin said.

Marcus and Roger agreed.

For the next hour or so, they continued making trips to the dumpster and the cars. As they got progressively drunker, they became ultra-minimalist.

Marcus came into the bedroom to find Robin staring at her mom's wedding dress spread across the bed. It looked like she'd been crying.

"I feel like I shouldn't throw this away," Robin said.

"Well … are you ever going to wear it?" Marcus said.

"I'm pretty sure it'd fall apart."

Marcus, his hands already full of stuff to throw away, said, "I mean, it's pretty sentimental. We can certainly find a way to store it."

Robin wiped away a tear and smiled in a way that made her look crazy.

"You know what?" she said. "Fuck it. If I'm starting over, I'm starting over."

"That's the spirit." Marcus gave her a quick peck on the lips before dumping his handful of stuff in the laundry cart and laughing. "I'll throw away all those old photo albums Grandma left me!"

"I'll get rid of my yearbooks."

"I've never had to use my high school diploma for anything!"

Roger just beamed and said, "I just love to see people getting rid of unnecessary things."

The three of them continued chucking stuff into the dumpster—their bedframe, most of their clothes, thousands of dollars' worth of abandoned hobbies—getting progressively drunker and laughing louder.

Eventually the only thing left in the apartment was the growler, its remains, and their three pint glasses. They carried them all down to the dumpster. Roger poured the remaining beer into their glasses and chucked the growler into the dumpster, where it shattered with a satisfying sound, even though he could have just as easily taken it home with him.

A large hairy man with no shirt on the third floor opened his window and shouted, "Would you keep it down!? I'm trying to sleep!"

"Oh, fuck off!" Robin yelled and flipped the guy off.

Roger laughed as the man slammed his window shut.

Marcus worried the man might come down and kick all of their asses.

Roger lit a cigarette and they all stood around the dumpster sipping their beers.

"There are, like, two whole lives in there," Marcus said.

"It's just stuff, man," Roger said.

"You're right," Marcus said.

"I feel so unburdened," Robin said. "Lighter."

"Me too," Marcus said.

"I'm still going home to a hoard." Roger sounded sad.

Roger lived a couple of blocks from their soon to be former apartment. He'd gotten a roommate after his girlfriend left. Marcus thought the roommate was a little off his rocker and possibly unhoused until Roger let him move in. It didn't take long for the roommate to fill the house with garbage. The last time they'd been over there, a pyramid of Pizza Hut boxes completely occluded the coffee table.

The three sipped their beer and watched the sun set over the city. When they were finished with their beers, they threw their glasses in the dumpster and went to the bar. The next morning, they drove their two loaded cars to the tiny house in Little Falls.

4

ROBIN HAD ONLY BEEN AWAKE a few seconds when she noticed the sounds. Judging by the light penetrating the curtain covering the tiny window in the loft, it had to be relatively early. She grabbed her phone, hoping it was early enough for her to close her eyes and try to get a bit more sleep.

8:32.

Good. She had another hour.

There was the sound again.

Thump.

Thump.

Followed by a scuffling sound.

Was someone on their roof?

She nudged Marcus. He'd been up late with Roger last night after the move. He licked the film from his lips and muttered something unintelligible.

"Do you hear that?" Robin said.

"Hm?"

"What is that sound?"

Marcus opened his eyes and cleared some crust from the corners. "Is ... someone on the roof?"

"That's what it sounds like."

"Maybe it's a squirrel or something."

"Squirrels don't make sounds like that."

Marcus rolled over on his stomach and pulled the curtain back on the window. "Peter's car's out there."

Robin rolled over onto her stomach to look, her heart skipping a beat as Peter's upside-down face filled the window. He was on the roof.

He tapped on the window. Robin pulled the thin blanket up over her shoulders as Marcus cracked the window.

"I knocked," Peter said. "No one answered. Hope I didn't wake you up. You know how I mentioned the lightning rod?"

"Uh, yeah, I guess," Marcus said.

"Well, I'm putting a placeholder up here to get an idea of how it looks. I won't be too much longer."

"Um, okay."

Robin had to pee really bad and wanted Marcus to close the curtain since they both slept in their underwear.

"You should come out and take a look when you get the chance," the landlord said.

"Sure," Marcus said.

"I'll let you guys get back to it." Peter's head lifted from the window's opening and they continued to hear the thumping and scuffling sounds.

Robin picked up her thin silk robe from the floor. In the apartment, she'd mostly wandered around naked because they were eight stories from the ground. Here, she felt too close to the street, too close to neighbors, and tried to stay covered up.

"I have to pee," she said.

"Yeah. Guess I'm going to go look at this stupid fucking lightning rod."

"Placeholder." Robin raised a finger before sliding out of bed.

"Right," Marcus said.

He put on a t-shirt and shorts, descended the absurd staircase, and went outside.

"I'm around back!" Peter called as though he'd been listening for someone to come out of the house.

Marcus went around back to join him.

Peter stood nearly at the back of the yard, looking up at the house. "What do you think?" he said.

Marcus turned to look at the house, surprised at the length of the wooden pole ascending from the roof. It reached at least fifty feet above the house. And … was it made of dowel rods duct-taped together? He was pretty sure it was.

"So this is going to be …"

"A lightning rod. I mean, I'm going to replace it with metal but … well, you get the idea."

"Yeah … Looks great, man. I'm sure it'll make us feel a lot safer." But he didn't know if that was correct. Truthfully, he was more confused by it than anything. He found himself looking at the rotting wood of the back porch and wondering why Peter wasn't doing something about that. It seemed like more of a priority than a lightning rod.

Peter began talking about lightning rods at length and Marcus wondered what century they were living in. It was too early for Marcus to pay attention to anything so he let Peter go on as long as he could take it before saying, "Robin probably has breakfast ready."

Peter kept talking.

Marcus said, "So I should probably go in and eat."

Peter kept talking.

Marcus began walking away from him.

Peter stopped talking abruptly. A dark look clouded his eyes.

"Go eat," he said. "I don't want to keep you from your breakfast. I know I can be a bit kooky at times."

Marcus wanted to tell him to call and let them know when he was going to be doing stuff around the house but he hated conflict and rationalized it probably wouldn't happen again. Besides, the rent was cheap and a minor inconvenience here and there was nothing to stress over.

Instead, he said, "No worries," and headed back to the house, feeling the landlord's eyes burning into him.

5

MARCUS TWISTED AND YANKED ON the doorknob of the backdoor but the door wouldn't budge. He could see Robin standing in front of the stove in her robe, cooking scrambled eggs. She seemed drowsy or lost in thought. He knocked lightly on the window of the door. Robin started and clenched the neckline of her robe as she stared at him wide-eyed before relaxing.

Marcus jiggled the doorknob to signal he was locked out. Robin took the few short steps down the hallway and unlocked the door. Marcus tried the door again but it still wouldn't budge.

"Pull the knob on your side," Marcus said.

Robin twisted and pulled on the knob on her side but the door wasn't opening. Marcus looked over his shoulder, about to ask the landlord if was some special technique he didn't know about to open the door, but the landlord was gone.

Marcus turned back to the door.

Robin shouted, as if he wouldn't be able to hear her through the single pane of glass, "It won't open!"

Marcus waved his hand at her. "Back up."

She complied.

Marcus twisted the knob and rammed his shoulder into the door. "Fuck!" Pain shot through his shoulder and down his arm. He took a step back and launched his whole body at the door. The decrepit wooden door broke free of its painted frame and slammed into the hallway wall, the glass rattling in its frame. Marcus landed in the hallway.

"Oh my god!" Robin said. "Are you okay?"

Marcus didn't want Robin to worry, even though he was sure he'd done something bad to his shoulder. "I'm fine. It's okay." He picked himself off the floor.

"Figured I might as well start breakfast. There was no way I was gonna fall back asleep after that. Dude's fucking creepy. Who works on anything before nine in the morning? And who goes around looking in people's bedroom windows?"

"I think the guy's autistic or something," Marcus said. "He just kept talking and wouldn't take the hint that I didn't want to spend half the day having a conversation about lightning rods."

Robin pulled the pan of eggs to a cold burner and shut off the gas stove. "It must be a thing in Little Falls." She opened a cupboard and retrieved two plates, scraped some eggs onto each one, and set them on the table before searching through the drawer for silverware.

"What do you mean?"

The kitchenette table was under one of the two downstairs windows facing the street. Robin set forks beside each plate and sat. Marcus followed her. She pointed out the window to the roof of the house across the street. That's when Marcus noticed the large lightning rod on top of the neighbor's house. He looked up and down the street. Every house he could see had the same lightning rod.

"Guess they get a lot of electrical storms here?" Robin asked, confused.

Marcus shrugged before taking a bite of his eggs. He swallowed the food before adding, "Maybe. There are a lot of big trees and small houses."

They ate in silence, both staring out the window. No traffic. No pedestrians. When they'd finished their meal Marcus collected the dishes and took them to the sink, ran some water on them to soak, and proceeded to dig around in the few boxes they'd brought with them the day before. He retrieved his coffee maker, far more superior than the Mr. Coffee sitting on the counter.

"What should I do with the old coffee pot?" Marcus said.

"Um, I think he said to set anything we don't want out at the curb."

Marcus unplugged the old device and set his stainless-steel coffee pot in its spot before walking the old coffee maker out to the curb.

When he walked back into the house, Robin was staring out the window, her mouth open. Marcus followed her line of sight to see that the coffee maker was already, miraculously, gone.

He gave a short laugh and said, "That was fast."

"I didn't even see where they came from. It was like … a raggedy person. They grabbed it and disappeared into the bushes between those two houses." She pointed at the two houses and their wildly overgrown shrubs.

"Probably some old hippie. I'm sure their aware of when new people move in. They were probably surveilling the place."

"Fucking weird."

"At least it's not going to waste."

Robin thought about the dumpsters they'd recently filled up and wondered if either of them really gave a shit about anything going to waste.

"True," she said.

She decided it was time to fire up the washer. She'd hoarded a week's worth of laundry before the move, not wanting to pay to use the decrepit machines in the apartment building. The pile was shoved into a large, black trash bag and she was certain it probably reeked of mildew. She'd shoved damp towels in the bag the morning of the move.

She thought, *No more pumping coins into shitty washers.*

She grabbed the trash bag and pulled it to the narrow gap between the stairs. Marcus proceeded to prepare his caffeine fix.

Robin assessed the washer and dryer situation. A small cutout, possibly a former closet, was situated behind the spiral staircase. It was the home of the top-loading washer and dryer. There wasn't much room to access the machines. And the stairs were an obstacle, forcing her to bend over the machines and shimmy under the stairs to reach them. She was unable to stand upright and smacked her head on a stair rung in the process of loading the washer.

"Fuck!" she yelled.

"You okay?" Marcus asked.

Robin rubbed her head. "Yeah. It's gonna take some time to get used to tiny living." She started the washer and shimmied back out from under the stairs. "It's a pain in the ass but it's better than going to the laundromat."

"We need tiny house helmets," Marcus said.

"Huh?"

"You know, if we keep hitting our heads."

"I really hope you're joking."

"We'll see."

They both sat in the gamer chairs in the living room, listening to the washer fill and the coffee pot sputter.

"What needs to be done around here?" Marcus asked.

"Guess we should figure out what stays and what goes. It'll probably be easier to put our stuff away once what we don't need is gone."

The coffee pot completed its cycle and Marcus rose to tend to it and pour himself a cup. The washer stopped filling with water and made the most horrendous noise as it began to agitate the clothes. The sound was loud and sounded like they were trying to wash Freddy Krueger's glove.

"Oh my god!" Robin shouted over the noise. "What the fuck is that?"

"It's the washer!" Marcus held his hands over his ears.

"Why is it so fucking loud?"

"I don't know!"

"Should we unplug it?"

"Probably! It sounds like it's gonna blow up!"

"That's normal!" another shouted voice interrupted.

Robin and Marcus turned toward the front door, which was now open, and the landlord stood in the threshold. He looked at both of them expectantly with a large goofy grin, as if he were waiting for them to continue the conversation. The couple seemed to be at a loss for words, both wondering why the landlord had decided to invite himself in.

Robin yelled, hesitantly, "I don't think that's normal!"

The landlord shrugged, "It works fine!"

"It may work!" Marcus shouted. "But that noise is not normal!"

"You can just go for a walk when you run it! That's what I did!"

"If we don't I think we're going to end up with permanent hearing damage!"

Robin shouted, "I think the washer needs serviced!"

The landlord's face fell. "You want me to buy a new washer!?"

"No! Call a repair person!"

Peter threw his arms up in defeat. "Fine! I guess I'll spend money replacing something that works!" He spun and stomped toward his car.

Robin and Marcus watched as he slid in behind the driver's seat, glared at them, and sped off down the street. Outside the house, the washer sounded as though someone was torturing a cat.

"Maybe we should go for a walk until the washer's done," Marcus said.

"It is a nice day. Might give us a chance to see some of the town." She looked down at her robe. "Guess I should get dressed."

"Let me grab some jars so I can catch some air."

6

STANDING IN THE MIDDLE OF a headshop, Marcus opened his jar to capture the scents of incense, diet weed, and old building while the clerk watched him cautiously. Marcus thought the town might agree with him. He screwed the cap on, scrawled down his time and location on a label, and slapped it on the jar. Robin slid another stick of incense into the store's pyramid of jars and glanced at Marcus. He was … smiling.

"What're you so happy about?" She moved closer to him.

"You saw what I just did, right?"

"Uh, yeah, you're never too covert about it."

"And nobody said anything."

"They probably think you're a crazy person. Plus, anytime someone asks you about it, you try to sell them a jar of bottled air."

He looked at the hippie girl sitting behind the counter, staring into the middle distance. "Oh, she's totally getting a card."

Robin rolled her eyes.

"What?" Marcus said. "Your knees are out. That's your business

24

card. People can't just, like, *see* air."

"Do you ever feel like a fraud?"

Marcus shook his head. "Never." He looked at her knees. "Do you ever feel like an exhibitionist? Just giving it away for free?"

"I never said I was modest."

"You should tattoo a QR code above your knees."

"The last thing I want is for creepy old men to openly upskirt me."

"Fair."

They bought ten sticks of incense so Marcus could have an excuse to place a small stack of his business cards on the counter after getting permission from the clerk, a very stoned girl with dreadlocks who didn't look old enough to be there. Predictably, she said it was okay. More specifically, she said, "Whatever, man."

"Captured Air ... Turning memories into adventure."

Across the street from the headshop, Marcus pulled out another jar and hovered it over a flowerbed outside a business that sold crystals and did psychic readings. He glanced back to see the headshop clerk leaning against the doorway of the store, staring at them. But Marcus would not be deterred until he'd held the jar open for at least thirty seconds.

He clapped the cap back on and screwed it shut, applied the label, and they continued their stroll around the town. Granted, it was a weekday, but it seemed incredibly empty despite having a touristy feel. The weather was perfect, the smell of blooming flowers and the sound of birdsong wrapping their walk in a peaceful ambience. It was so much different than the growling buildings, shrieking bus brakes, blaring car horns, and all-pervasive thrum of the city.

While it was evident from the shops and restaurants the town had money, it also looked like it had seen better days.

"Looks like this whole town could use a fresh coat of paint," Robin said.

"I think it's charming. Unpretentious. Almost rustic."

The downtown area was only about four blocks, although they weren't really conventional blocks. Two main streets came together, the road the headshop was on terminating as it connected to the state route. A bike path hub was to the north, a state park was to the east, and the heart of downtown was to the south. They went in that direction. After about a half mile, they were back in a residential area.

"A-a-a-nd that's the town," Robin said.

"Quaint," Marcus said.

"It could be a lot worse. We know there's a brewery. Big bonus. But I counted two bars, at least five restaurants, a grocery store, three bookstores, and a record store. Not like the town where I lived."

"It's surprising, for sure."

"And … a laundromat for when the perfectly fine washing machine doesn't do such a fine job."

"I'm sure he'll fix or replace it."

"Really? Has that been your experience with renting?"

"Well … no."

"And if he does replace it, it'll be another piece of shit he found on the side of the road."

They made a right and walked for a couple of blocks until they came to their street, where they made another right and headed home. From a block away, they could hear the washer. Then it stopped.

"Cycle must be finished," Robin said. "Good timing. That sound is embarrassing."

"I'm not closing the windows just so we can do laundry."

Robin laughed a little. "I'm with you. Your irritating dog is our obnoxiously loud washer that probably doesn't clean the clothes."

As if on cue, a large black dog bounded from behind a house to their right, throwing itself into the fence in a rattle of metal and barking ferociously. They both jumped.

"Jesus fucking Christ." Robin put a hand on her pounding heart.

"At least they don't live very long," Marcus said. "That one looked like it had five years, tops."

They reached their house and went inside. A pile of wet laundry sat in the middle of the floor upon a blue tarp.

"What's this shit?" Robin said.

Marcus, pointing out the blue tarp, said, "At least his precious floor's safe."

He turned to place the incense on the table and spotted a note or letter or something on it. It was a full page of neatly printed handwriting. Marcus read it. It sounded vaguely poetic and barroom philosophical with an underlying unhinged quality that made Marcus easily picture Peter crying while he wrote it, probably while muttering to himself. But it contained information he found vital.

"It's replaced," Marcus said. "He said he didn't reload our clothes because he didn't want to be intrusive or creepy. He put 'creepy' in quotes."

"You heard the washer stop when I did, right?"

"Yeah."

"How could he have replaced it that fast?"

"Maybe we heard something else."

"Really? Because that was the exact sound it was making when we left. And then he has time to write a fucking full-page letter?"

Robin stalked over to the washer.

"If he replaced it," she said. "It's the exact same model."

"Yeah. He's a landlord. I'm sure it's just the cheapest of the cheap. Looks new."

"So did the last one."

"Well, maybe he just fixed it."

Robin began scooping up the pile of wet clothes and jamming them in the washer, negotiating the bulky staircase.

"We'll see," she said. She grabbed another armload and shouted "Fuck!" as she clonked her head on the staircase.

"*Tiny house helmet*," Marcus sang.

He grabbed up the last of the garments and waited for Robin to come out of the laundry cave before going in himself, hitting his head and also shouting, "Fuck!"

Robin waited for him to vacate the space before moving in and turning it on.

It was quiet.

7

MARCUS AND ROBIN WERE NAPPING in the loft when Robin woke to the sound of her stomach growling. She was hungry and reached for her phone to check the time. The clock on her phone read 6:03 PM. She groaned.

Marcus responded to her groan with one of his own. "What time is it?"

"A little after six. I'm starving."

"I brought a frozen lasagna from the apartment. Probably need to get rid of it anyway. That refrigerator is really small. I don't know if we'd be able fit a frozen pizza in the freezer or not."

Robin sat up and pulled her robe on. "I'll go preheat the oven." She managed to bang her head on the ceiling as she descended the stairs. "Fuck! I swear I'm going to end up with brain damage from this house."

"Eventually muscle memory will kick in. Until then, might I recommend—"

"Don't fucking say it."

"Tiny house helmet," he whispered through clenched teeth.

"One day I'm going to marry you just so I can divorce you."

Robin assessed the oven. She wasn't sure the stove was even two feet wide on the outside, and when she opened the oven door the space inside was laughable. There was no way she could make a Thanksgiving turkey in the thing. She moved one of the racks to the center of the oven and turned it on to preheat. She just hoped the damn thing worked and didn't make a horrible sound like the washer. The memory of a decrepit stove in an old apartment, when she was barely twenty, came back to haunt her. She'd tried to make a pumpkin pie in the old stove but it just wouldn't bake. After three hours in the oven, which felt hot to her, the center of the pie was still liquid. She hoped this oven worked better than the one from her memory. This one looked fairly new at least.

She pulled the lasagna from the freezer. Marcus was right. There was no way a pizza was fitting in the freezer. If they wanted pizza, they'd have to buy one to bake as soon as they got home or order one.

Robin dug around in the cabinets until she found a baking sheet to set the lasagna on and preemptively placed it in the oven. She waited for the stove to signal it was ready before setting a timer.

While waiting, she snapped a few photos of her knees next to the lasagna box. The photos weren't really her thing but she was certain someone would buy them. She once got a sizeable payment for rubbing peanut butter on her knees and taking a couple quick shots. She was uploading the photos when Marcus called down.

"What are you doing?" Marcus said. "Why is it so hot in here?"

"I'm just preheating the oven."

"Well, it feels like an oven up here."

Robin approached the appliance. It did feel hot near it but what oven didn't when it was on? She flipped the switch for the range exhaust to blow the hot air outside. While her hand was on the exhaust switch she could feel a blast of hot air. She waved her hand above the appliance door and found the source of the hot air. The door to the oven was either warped or the thing might have been dropped. There was a substantial gap where the door did not close all the way. She flipped the light switch for the oven and could clearly see light through the gap.

"It's getting hotter!" Marcus yelled. "I'm gonna cook!" He panted, crawled to the stairs, and knocked his head on the ceiling as he descended. "Fuck!"

"I turned the exhaust fan on," Robin said. "But I think the oven door is broken. Take a look at this."

Marcus crossed the two steps from the end of the stairs to the range. Robin pointed at the large gap in the door. Marcus inspected it and the range exhaust and sighed.

"The exhaust doesn't vent outdoors." He placed his hands in front of the vertical slits on the range hood. "It's one of those recirculating hoods."

"What's the point of that?"

"Don't know. To make your ceiling all greasy I guess." He pointed to the large yellowish stain on the ceiling, in the same spot the exhaust was blowing.

"The range is gas. Aren't you supposed to vent it outside. Seems dangerous."

"I'm sure there's some sort of building code or a loophole Peter found to get around it."

"Regardless, the stove is fucked." Robin pushed on the oven door, attempting to make the gap smaller.

"It's roasting upstairs. We'll have to let him know."

Robin groaned. "Not that guy. He creeps me out. Besides, he didn't seem too happy that he had to replace the washer."

Someone whistled a low two-tone tune outside. The couple gave each other a confused look. The whistler sounded closer to their house than they both cared for. The whistle came again. Marcus and Robin turned to the window beside the refrigerator. Robin jumped when she realized Peter was standing in the flowerbed under the window and staring at them with a huge grin, unmoving.

"Hi!" the landlord nearly shouted. "Have you seen my cat? This has been his home the last few months while I was making repairs. I'm pretty sure he might have made his way back here." He stared at them, unblinking and smiling.

"Oh, uh," Robin said. "I haven't seen a cat."

"Don't let him in if you see him."

"Okay," Marcus said. "We won't. I'm glad you're here. We're having an issue with the ov—"

"His name is Skirt. He's thirty-five years old. I found him when he was a kitten. I built that cat house for him. I checked it but he wasn't there."

Robin said, "Cat house?"

"Yeah," the landlord said. "The one that matches the house in the tree line."

The couple looked at each other, confused. Neither of them remembered seeing a cat house.

"I can send you a text if we happen to see him," Robin said.

"Skirt," Peter said.

"Skirt," Robin repeated.

The landlord continued to stare at them, smiling. The beat of awkwardness went on for too long before Marcus interrupted it.

"As I was saying, the oven is broken."

"Broken?" Peter said. "I just had that delivered a month ago."

"Well, it takes twice as long to cook anything and it makes the loft a boiler room."

Peter's eyes went blank before a shudder rippled through him. It looked insectoid. He backed away from the house and turned toward the front door. Peter let himself into the house.

"There's an air conditioner in the window up there," Peter said, pointing toward the loft.

"Yeah. But we don't want to have to turn the air conditioner on if we don't want to."

A cloud of rage descended on Peter's face. He stamped his foot, rattling everything in the tiny house. "It's brand new!"

Marcus's heart picked up its pace. He took a deep breath and thought about the best air he'd ever captured. He moved toward the stove and pulled open the oven door.

"Look, dude. Here, where the door is bent ... It's not even creating a seal. It's wasteful."

Peter kicked the door closed, enraged.

Robin jumped. She scuttled a few steps away from the landlord, about as far away from him as she could get in the tiny house, palms facing out in a defensive gesture. Angry men had always frightened her.

"Fine!" He threw up his skinny arms. "You want a new stove, I'll get you a new stove. I'm a pretty great landlord."

The self-serving platitude seemed to light him up. His eyes brightened and that crazy smile again twisted his lips. He approached the stove and began tugging it out from the wall.

Robin grabbed a pot holder, opened the oven, and retrieved their dinner.

"I can help you take it out to the curb," Marcus said. "We have a hand truck."

"That'd be great. But I'm not leaving it at the curb. I paid too much for it."

"I'll get the hand truck," Robin said, eager to remove herself from the situation.

~

Marcus and Peter breathed heavily after getting the small stove through the small door. The appliance was still hot and Marcus had a hard time getting a grip on the contraption with pot holders on his hands. Peter had asked for a marker and a piece of paper so he could write "DON'T TAKE" and tape it to the stove.

"I have to go get my trailer," Peter said.

Peter lived two minutes away, so Marcus didn't understand why he sounded so put out.

"Thanks a lot," Marcus said.

"I should be able to get my hands on a new one pretty quickly."

"That'd be great."

"Go eat your dinner. I'll be back in a bit."

Marcus went back into the house. Robin had sliced the lasagna and divided it between two plates. Marcus opened a bag of chips and filled the empty half of his plate. They sat at the table, eating their half-cooked dinner.

"That guy …" Robin said.

"I know," Marcus said. "He's a bit much. Maybe we'll get things ironed out and he'll go away."

"I don't want to be here when he comes back."

"Okay. Yeah, we've still got an hour or so of daylight left. Want to take a small hike and see if Roger's at the brewery? I could use a beer."

"Sounds like a plan."

8

ROGER WAS ALONE BEHIND THE bar. He perked up when he spotted Marcus and Robin.

"Hey, folks," Roger said. "What can I get you?"

"What do you recommend?" Marcus said.

"I like the Square Tire. It's an imperial IPA. It'll make you feel different."

"Sounds amazing," Marcus said. "I'll have that."

Robin wrinkled her nose. "Do you have anything … less imperial?"

Roger looked at the chalkboard beer list. This was the first time Marcus had been in the brewery and it was the most modern thing he'd seen in Little Falls. Polished concrete floor. Exposed duct work. Light, gleaming wood surfaces and a lot of stainless steel. He heaved an inward sigh of relief when he noticed no TVs or pool tables. He'd always thought a bar should be a place to lose yourself in and surround yourself by people who wanted to do the same. He'd always found televised sports and competitive things like pool to be divisive.

Americans could find anything to fight over.

"Maybe the Farmhouse Workhouse Ale?" Roger said. "It's only 4.2. Pretty light. Based on a recipe the owner found when he took over the place. He liked to keep his employees drunk but not too drunk to work."

"That sounds good," Robin said.

Roger poured the beers and brought them over. Marcus proffered his credit card but Roger shrugged it off.

"You just moved here. First one's free. I can get you a flight if you want to try a bit of everything."

"Even ... more amazing," Marcus said.

Robin took a sip of her beer, perked up a bit, and said, "Hey, why's there a goat out front?"

Roger smiled. "That's Pan. He belongs to Jeremiah. He's out on a smoke break. The goat doesn't like to leave his side. They're ... pretty close, I guess."

"This place keeps getting weirder and weirder ..." Marcus said.

"Good weird or bad weird?" Roger asked.

Marcus held up a hand and let it wobble back and forth a bit. Robin serenely closed her eyes and shook her head softly.

"New place not working out?"

"The place is great, other than it being, you know, tiny. But the landlord ..."

"Oh boy ..." Robin said, taking a more robust sip of her beer.

A guy they assumed was Jeremiah slid in the back door and behind the counter as both Marcus and Robin harangued Roger with what had happened with the landlord since moving in. A mere glimpse of Jeremiah had Marcus immediately fascinated. This guy had to be a character. His first thought was that it looked like he'd wandered in from some fantastic shire. He was short, with long, thinning red hair and an unkempt, bushy beard to match. He wore a brown leather vest over a black tank top. His shorts extended to just below his knees and the hair covering his shins and calves made Marcus think he may have been part goat himself. He didn't wear shoes and his hobbit feet were hairy with longer than usual toenails.

"This is Jeremiah," Roger said. "This is my brother, Marcus, and his girlfriend, Robin."

They shook hands with Jeremiah.

"They just moved to that tiny house on Hafford Street."

"Oh," Jeremiah said. "You rent from Peter?"

"Yeah," Marcus said. "You know him?"

"He comes in every now and then," Jeremiah said. "He owns most of the houses here."

"Really?" Robin said.

Jeremiah flicked a finger toward the ceiling. "No shit. You see a lightning rod on top of the house, he owns it. It's like his brand."

"What the fuck is it with the lightning rods?" Marcus said. "When we signed the lease, it seemed like the only thing he was concerned about."

"People have their theories, but I guess no one really knows."

Roger turned his back to pour their flight.

"How long have you lived here?" Marcus asked Jeremiah.

"My whole life."

Marcus tried to convince himself Jeremiah didn't look haunted when he said that.

"You must have some stories."

"Oh yeah."

"How long have you worked here?"

"Since it opened about ten years ago."

"More stories."

"You bet."

It was only a little after eight. It was a weeknight, so the patronage remained sparse. Marcus and Robin spent the next couple hours drinking and telling Roger and Jeremiah about their adventures in the new place. Every now and then Pan would *bah* from outside and Jeremiah would have to go out and do something to calm it down. He said the owner told him he could keep bringing Pan to work as long as he didn't become a nuisance.

Marcus was hoping to stay longer to get some landlord and town gossip from Jeremiah, but Robin checked her phone and said, "Hey, we should go. Big storm's on the way." She showed Marcus her phone, swirling masses of red and green barreling toward the village.

"Yeah, we'll take off."

He gave his card to Roger and settled the tab. They'd gone well beyond the complimentary first beers.

"Nice to meet you, Jeremiah. I'm sure we'll come back." Marcus looked at Roger and said, "Feel free to stop by before you head home. Any time."

"Thanks. I'll let you know."

Marcus and Robin stepped out of the bar and glanced over at Pan, bucking up and down by the dumpster under the safety light.

As if on cue, the wind picked up and thunder rumbled in the distance. They knew it would take them about fifteen minutes to walk home. They quickened their pace. The brewery abutted the bike path and the state park, so it seemed exceptionally dark on this end of town. Their tiny house was located almost dead center of the village proper, although most of the shops and businesses were in this quadrant.

A large crack of thunder caused them both to jump and stumble a bit. Marcus was a little tipsier than he thought he would be. Lightning turned the world around them bright.

"Holy shit," Marcus said as calmly as possible.

They continued walking in their rapid clip.

"What is it?" Robin said.

Marcus, not wanting to pause, pointed up above the canopy of trees covering nearly the entire town. "Keep watching when the lightning flashes again."

They heard the rain before they felt it, pouring down on them, cold but not uninviting in the steamy night.

Another deafening crack of thunder, this one expected.

"Wait for it," Marcus said.

Again, the sky lit up in that fabulous white-purple and, like skeletal hands reaching down from the heavens, the lightning connected with all the lightning rods reaching above the trees.

"*Wow* ..." Robin said. "It'd be really cool if it wasn't so ..."

"Horrifying?"

She laughed softly. "Yeah, I guess."

The wind picked up again and they walked even faster. They took their sandals off and carried them. Sticks and leaves smacked against them before they finally broke out into a jog. Neither of them was very athletic and they thought an outright run might kill them. They got closer to the tiny house, nervous about the giant tree covering the entire front yard. From the road, you wouldn't know the house was there until you were right up on it. They watched a bolt of lightning connect with the rod on their roof and this somehow made them feel more secure. They quickly sloshed through the front yard, let themselves in the house, and slammed the door behind them. The house was mercifully dry and oddly quiet. They peeled off their wet clothes, clambered up the weird staircase, and fucked until their rain-chilled skin was hot to the touch.

Somewhere outside, amidst the dying rumbles of the storm, they heard a cat's worried meow.

They were asleep within minutes of finishing.

9

"I THINK THAT LIGHTNING STRIKE blew the light bulbs in the bathroom," Robin said to Marcus as he descended the stairs and wiped the sleep from his eyes. She set plates full of hot breakfast foods on the table and took a seat.

Marcus stood by the table and did a double-take, looking back and forth at the food and the stove. "Is that new?" He pointed at the stove.

Robin sighed. "Yeah. And the stove at the curb is gone."

"Did he ... bring it while I was asleep?"

"While *we* were asleep."

"I'm not crazy, right? There was no stove when we got home last night."

"Nope. But there was one when I woke up. You gotta tell that guy if we're home we have to be awake if he wants to come in and do something to the place."

"Me? Why do I have to tell him?"

"Because that dude has some serious creep factor. I don't know what it is but he makes my skin crawl. Like, who the fuck delivers and hooks up a stove while tenants are sleeping!? And why is it the exact same stove!? Just like it was the exact same washer! Why am I yelling!?"

Marcus threw up his hands in surrender. "Okay, okay. The next time we see him I'll say something." Marcus slid into his chair to enjoy his breakfast. "You said something about the bathroom lights?"

"Yeah," she said around a bite of eggs. "I think that lightning strike last night might've blown the bulbs. At least that's what I hope the problem is. I don't want to have Peter come back over. After breakfast I was gonna walk up to the hardware store and get some new light bulbs."

"I'll come with you. I can capture some air there. I'm sure there are some men out there that relish the smell of a hardware store."

Robin nodded. "I can take some photos of my knees beside some tools too."

After the couple had finished their breakfast Marcus grabbed a tote and placed a few jars in it before they strolled to the hardware store. It was located on the corner where a side street "T"ed into the main street of town. Robin stopped short when she rounded the corner. Marcus copied her. They both stared at the rickety, hand-made, wood, a-frame sign on the sidewalk outside the hardware store. A nearly illegible scrawl boasted "Comedy Show 8 PM tonite!"

"This is …" Robin said, craning her head to look at the sign on the window that plainly stated "Hardware." "The hardware store, right?"

They both looked in the large windows. Half the store was empty except for rows of chairs. The other half of the small store contained a long shelf that ran from the front of the store to the back. The shelf and the wall behind it appeared to be crammed with stuff.

"I guess," Marcus said.

A man with long, dark hair and an unkempt beard poked his head out from behind the shelf at the back of the store. As soon as he spotted Robin and Marcus, an uneasy smile filled his face. Until the man spotted them Robin was contemplating running to the Dollar General on the edge of town. Something about the hardware store setup made her a little uneasy, like it was a front for something sinister she didn't want any part of.

The man inside started down the aisle, assuming they were about to enter. He was shirtless and shoeless but wore an extremely worn pair of jeans and a pristine new apron.

Marcus opened the door of the store for Robin and they entered.

"Hey, folks!" The man waved at them as he approached. "Name's Charlie. Are you here to buy tickets to the comedy show? The show actually starts at seven-thirty and I'll be performing a one-man show at eight. Tickets are only ten dollars each."

"Um …" Robin looked at Marcus.

Marcus thought the guy's name was fitting as he looked like Charles Manson's cousin. "We're actually here to purchase some light bulbs. I think last night's storm caused a few to blow."

"Really? Do you guys live here in town? I've never seen you before. I'm pretty sure I've seen everyone who lives here. I think I know everyone."

Marcus thought the guy seemed a little off but harmless. "We just moved here not too long ago."

"Where do you live?"

The hairs on Robin's neck rose. It was girl instinct to not give out any personal information to a man she just met—her eyes fell on his bare feet—especially one that didn't seem stable.

Marcus answered, "We moved into the tiny house on Hafford."

"Ohhhhhhhhhh." Charlie nodded slowly. "I know the place. Robin's egg blue with a cat house in the tree line. That's a Slager house, right? Peter Slager. He comes in here often. He just picked up a new stove this morning."

"The old stove was messed up," Robin said, hoping the guy wouldn't remember which house they'd moved into. She had the irrational thought she might wake up with Charlie in their house.

Marcus looked around the small store, searching for where they might've kept the large appliances, and contemplated asking Charlie what his hours were, since Peter had to have delivered the stove in the early hours of the morning.

Robin said, "Do you have any light bulbs? Preferably LED."

Charlie stared at her for a beat, as if he were searching his brain for the inventory of the store, before he smiled broadly and answered, "We have regular incandescent bulbs, but no LED."

"Incandescent will work," Marcus said.

"Be right back." Charlie walked back down the aisle before rounding the corner at its end and disappearing.

"Strange ranger," Robin said.

Marcus approached the counter that housed the cash register. He set his tote on the counter and proceeded to pull each jar from the tote and unscrew the lids.

Robin hurried over to the wall of tools and snapped a couple of quick photos of her knees with the instruments in the background. She didn't know why, but she didn't want Charlie to know what she did. She got the feeling the guy might have a knee fetish and she didn't like meeting her fans or potential fans in the wild. Especially if they knew where she lived.

Marcus was finishing up when Robin rejoined him.

"These should go quick for Father's Day." Marcus screwed the lid on the last jar and Robin helped him bag them up.

A loud crash came from the basement and they heard Charlie's feet slapping against the steps as he charged up them. Emerging at the top of the stairway, he looked nervous. Robin and Marcus waited at the counter. Charlie ran his fingers through his greasy hair before setting the lightbulb down.

"Looks like I just have the one."

The lightbulb was a brand neither of them had heard of. The packaging was caked in dust and it looked like it was from the nineties, at the latest.

"We'll take it," Marcus said.

Charlie wrote a product number in a notebook and said, "That'll be thirty even."

Robin audibly scoffed. Marcus did his best to keep his mouth from falling open. He hated haggling in all forms, but the price seemed outrageously steep. For thirty dollars they could buy a decade's worth of light bulbs.

"That's … a bit much, isn't it?"

Charlie kept tapping the lightbulb with his finger, the insane crooked smile back on his face.

"Well, this one's a vintage bulb. They don't really make 'em like this anymore. And I threw on twenty bucks for tickets to the comedy show. New to town, you're gonna want to meet everybody, aren't you?"

Lost, Marcus looked at Robin.

She rolled her eyes. "Just pay it," she mumbled.

"You guys are gonna love it," Charlie said.

Marcus handed him his credit card, wishing he had cash because he knew, somehow, even in this modern year, this would be a process. Paying for something with a card at a small business sometimes equated to the same feeling as writing a check at the grocery store. It made you feel like a major inconvenience. Thank a higher power that checks were nearly obsolete, unless you were over the age of seventy.

He was surprised when Charlie adeptly plugged a card reader into his phone.

"There's a ten percent fee for cards," he said.

"Of course there is," Marcus replied.

Charlie scanned the card and handed it back to Marcus.

"Is it possible to get a receipt?"

Charlie waved him away. "Nah, I'll remember you bought it if it gives you any problems." He raised a dirty finger. "But it won't. It'll probably be the best lightbulb you've ever used."

"Thanks," Marcus said, even though he didn't feel thankful. He felt like he'd been fleeced.

"Y'all have a good one," Charlie said. Then he pointed at them in succession and said, "Andy and Carrie, right?"

"Close," Marcus said and laughed. "I don't think we told you our names. I'm Marcus and she's Robin."

"Well, welcome to town. I can't wait to see you at the show tonight."

"Oh, yeah, do we need the tickets?"

Charlie just pointed at his head.

"Right," Marcus said. "You'll remember."

"See ya." Robin was already heading for the door.

Outside the hardware store, Marcus let out a massive sigh as they rounded the corner and headed home.

"Maybe it'll be fun," Robin said.

"We're actually going?"

"We paid for it."

"Not by choice."

"I'm sure you could have said you didn't want them."

"That would have just made things uncomfortable."

"It'll be a good opportunity for you to hand out some business cards. If you can sell some locally, think about how much you'll save in shipping."

"I guess. Jesus, what if Peter's there?"

"I didn't think about that. Maybe he'll be less weird in a social setting."

Marcus just looked at her and they shared a laugh.

10

MARCUS AND ROBIN LAY IN bed after waking up from their nap, still in the mellow thrall of the tail end of the edibles they'd consumed before dinner. Marcus napped in only his underwear, while Robin wore one of his old loose-fitting t-shirts. Marcus placed a hand on her stomach and said, "I want to eat your pussy."

Robin smiled lazily and said, "I'm not going to stop you."

He slid the t-shirt up her thighs and over her underwear, rolling between her legs to kiss her lower stomach as he hooked his fingers into the band of her panties.

Clearly, a cat meowed. The downstairs windows were open and it almost sounded like it was in the house.

Marcus slid Robin's underwear down her legs and tossed them off the bed.

He spread her apart and began licking and suckling her, her soft moans of pleasure mingling with the increasingly fevered cat's meow.

Then they heard the whistling.

Robin placed her hand on the top of his head and pushed him

away from her.

"He's here," she hissed.

"Well, I don't think he's coming in."

"You don't know that. The door's unlocked. It's not like he hasn't let himself in before. Besides, you need to go talk to him."

"About what?"

Robin's eyes went wide and Marcus could tell she was biting back her anger. "About him fucking coming in here while we're asleep!"

"Oh, yeah."

Marcus slid to the foot of the bed and pulled his shorts on over his hard-on. He pulled a t-shirt on and crawled to the stairs before scuttling down them and hitting his head on something.

"Fuck!"

He saw the cat before he saw the landlord. It was clawing at the screen and meowing at memories or something. It didn't even look alive. Missing one eye and half its tail, it looked like an ancient and wildly abused stuffed toy. He took a deep breath to try and center himself before opening the door and stepping outside just as Peter was entering the yard to retrieve his cat.

"Hey, Art," Peter said.

"It's Marcus," Marcus said.

"Right. I'll get it eventually. What's up?"

"I didn't want to say anything but, you know, you being in the place at night while we're asleep is really freaking Robin out."

"Oh, you mean when I installed the brand-new oven in a timely fashion, completing a request made to me in person?"

"Yeah, man. Thanks, for sure, but you have to let us know you're going to be in there. We need our privacy."

Marcus watched a bolt of anger light Peter's eyes before he bit it back and plastered on that crazy grin, his eyes returning to that of a deranged guru.

"Duly noted," he said. "I'm just here retrieving Skirt. Hopefully you don't report me for trespassing." He reached down to retrieve the cat and Marcus almost felt sorry for saying anything. "Come on, buddy. I don't think we're wanted here."

Maybe Peter was oversensitive. Marcus certainly wasn't going to press him into a full-fledged argument. He turned and went back into the house without saying anything else. He was pretty sure he heard Peter fart before exiting the yard.

11

"DO YOU THINK," MARCUS BEGAN, "that ten dollars for a half-hour local comedy show followed by a one-man show from the guy who works at the hardware store is a bit expensive?"

"Everything's expensive. That's why we jumped at the chance to live in a glorified shed for eight hundred a month."

"I guess. Should have brought my jars. The air from a hardware store is one thing. The air from a hardware store slash comedy club is something else entirely."

"Maybe it'll be fun."

"I'll try to have a good time."

It was a nice evening. They walked on a sidewalk that had seen better days under a canopy of catalpa, oaks, and maples. The air was filled with birdsong and the soothing hum of crickets and katydids. In the distance, dogs barked and children played. He pulled Robin's hand into his as they continued walking to the hardware store.

From the way Charlie talked it up, he half expected to see a line out the door. But of course there wasn't a line. The door was propped open and Robin could see there were about seven people in there, at most. They were all ancient. She was pretty sure it was the same group of olds she'd seen sitting in front of the senior citizen center the couple of times they'd been on Main Street.

Whatever hopes Marcus had for the show must have completely dissipated because he muttered, "This is gonna suck so bad," before entering the store.

"It'll probably be an hour, at most. Then maybe we can hit the brewery if you're up for it." When all else failed, she figured beer was probably the way to his heart.

He smiled. "You have me all figured out."

There were maybe twenty-five old wooden folding chairs. They pretty much had their pick of them but chose to sit in the second row. Marcus wanted to sit in back in case they needed to make a quick escape, but Robin dragged him closer to the "stage," which was three wood pallets with plywood boards thrown over them.

Marcus plopped down heavily in his chair and said, "It still smells exactly like a hardware store."

The olds—four men and three women—all turned to look at them. They gave polite smiles and seemed pleasant enough. Robin expected them to start trying to talk to them, but Charlie stumbled onto the stage before anyone could say anything.

Charlie seemed either exceptionally drunk, exceptionally high, or both.

Even though she was sure Charlie knew every attendee by name, he addressed the crowd as though it were a sold-out theater.

"Hey, folks, thanks so much for coming. My name's Charlie Osborne and I'll be your MC for the evening. We've got a good line-up of comics and don't forget to stick around for the debut of my one-man show, 'Nesting Man'. I think you're really gonna like it."

The olds clapped and Marcus and Robin followed suit.

"Now please give a warm Little Falls welcome, all the way from North Southwest College Street, Rachel Rackem!"

More applause.

A mousy, dark-haired girl who couldn't have been out of high school stumbled as she attempted to take the stage.

"Thanks for letting me out of my cage, Charlie." She smirked to laughter and light applause. It was the last interesting thing she said. She spent the next five minutes telling the kinds of jokes Robin thought every comedian knew not to do. It wasn't that they were racist or sexist or transphobic or anything. They were just bad. Like the kinds of jokes she remembered reading in joke books as a child. Worse than dad jokes. The type of jokes that made you want to groan when you heard them. Nevertheless, they continued feigning laughter and applause throughout the painful duration of her mercifully short set.

When she was finished she disappeared into the doorway that led to the basement. Robin thought she would probably reemerge to watch the rest of the acts, but she never did. Maybe the thing about Charlie keeping her in a cage wasn't a joke at all. Maybe it was his daughter. She didn't see anyone else in attendance who could have been the right age to be her parents. This seemed like the kind of town where all the parents were supportive enough to attend anything their child did.

Charlie took the stage.

"Rachel Rackem everybody!" He seemed out of breath. "Our next act is really something special. All the way from Family Acres Rest Home, please give it up for Naomi Injeera!"

A very old woman used her cane to attempt the stage, then gave it up and simply stood in front of it. It put her uncomfortably close to the people in the front row. They began gradually edging their seats back, forcing Robin and Marcus to do the same.

Naomi's thin white hair still retained a few dreadlocks and she dressed in hippie garb and smelled like patchouli and nursing home.

"Thanks, uh …" She laughed. "Welp, I done forgot his name." She smiled. She didn't have many teeth. "Now let's get down to business."

She spent the next ten minutes skewering the patriarchy and fighting to catch her breath. Robin thought it was hilarious and she could feel Marcus shaking with laughter next to her. She found herself genuinely thinking the night might not suck after all. When Naomi's act dissolved into a coughing fit and she wandered outside to either lose a lung or die, things took a turn for the worse.

Charlie took the stage once again, but his mood seemed darker.

"Well, everyone, that was … oops, I can't seem to remember her name." He shot a death glare at the door.

"Wun't that yer meemaw?" one of the older women in the front asked.

Charlie hissed at her like a cat. Robin wasn't sure she'd ever seen or heard another human actually hiss at someone before.

THE LANDLORD

"Anyway, let me apologize for that. The next time, we'll try to make sure we get people who are a little funnier. Okay, now for our final act. All the way from Lord Street, you know him, you love him, he owns my house and he probably owns yours—"

"Jesus fuuucking Christ," Robin muttered as Marcus sigh-groaned noticeably.

"Peter Slager!"

Peter took the stage like he'd done it a million times before. He seemed comfortable and likable. He received more genuine applause than the previous two performers.

"Thank you, thank you, Charlie. It's nice to see some gratitude. You know, gratitude's an interesting thing. It's so easy for most but so *hard* for some. It should be easy. The easiest thing in the world. Someone does something nice for you and you say thanks. Or you return the favor. It's the social contract. It's just how things work. But some people don't seem to know what that is." He shot daggers at Marcus and Robin and Robin could sense a rant coming on. He pointed to an old man in the front row. "You, old wizard, if I were to bring … let's say an oven to your house and hook it up for you so that you woke up in the morning to find this shiny, new, beautiful thing in your kitchen, what would you say?"

"Well, I'd sure say thanks."

"Exactly." He looked at them again.

"Fuck this," Robin said. She grabbed Marcus's hand and they both stood up and began walking toward the front door. Robin felt Marcus fidgeting.

"There he goes," Peter said. "Probably has the shits again."

The olds burst out in raucous laughter.

At the door, Marcus yanked his hand out of his pocket and slapped down a small stack of business cards on a local promo table by the door.

They were at least a block away before either of them could summon the air to speak.

"I think that was the right move," Marcus said.

"I don't care what it takes," Robin said. "We're getting out of that lease as soon as possible. Even if I have to start doing nudes."

"I think I need *all* the beer."

They continued walking to the brewery amidst the impressive pink and purple sunset their rage prevented them from noticing.

12

PAN TURNED HIS HEAD SIDEWAYS, opened his mouth, and let his tongue flop about as he yelled and snorted at Marcus and Robin when they approached the brewery. He was tied to the bike rack beside the entrance and stood on his hind legs before dropping onto all fours, blathering like an idiot the entire time.

"I'm pretty sure that thing is possessed," Marcus said as he opened the door for Robin.

Robin laughed at Pan and said, "Pretty sure that's how I feel right now."

Jeremiah marched past them as they entered. They both assumed he would take care of Pan since the animal seemed to have gone bonkers.

Roger looked up from his phone as they approached the bar. There were only a handful of people drinking in the establishment.

Marcus thumbed over his shoulder toward the door. "That goat is nuts. Have you seen how it's acting?"

"It gets like that sometimes," Roger said. "What can I get for you?"

"A new place to live," Robin said.

"That bad, huh?"

"Even worse," Marcus said.

"The usual?"

"Sure."

Roger turned to pour two beers for them. While he was busy, Jeremiah entered the brewery and slipped behind the bar. He looked sweaty and aggravated.

Robin asked Jeremiah, "Do you know of any rentals in town that Peter Slager doesn't own?"

Marcus spotted another customer sitting at the bar alone. The patron lifted his head a little as if their conversation had piqued his interest or, maybe, Marcus thought, *I might be a bit paranoid after the evening's events.*

Jeremiah scratched his chin. "I can't think of any at the moment. You'll be hard pressed to find anything Peter doesn't own."

"Where could we find available rentals?" Marcus asked. "Besides the online newspaper."

Roger set two pint glasses in front of the couple. "I've heard it's mainly word of mouth around here. You gotta know someone who knows someone type of thing. Right?" Roger looked at Jeremiah.

"I guess you could try the MyFace groups. I've heard there are some that post freebies and rentals in town. I don't know for sure though. I don't have social media. I don't even own a phone. I just hear about this stuff from drunk people."

Robin retrieved her phone from her back pocket and began searching MyFace groups.

"We have to move as soon as possible," Marcus said. "We'd like to stay in Little Falls. We like the town a lot. But we just can't take Peter anymore."

Without looking up from her phone, Robin said, "He's fucking creepy, invasive, and a condescending asshole."

"That's a tall order," Jeremiah said.

"Did something else happen?" Roger said.

Marcus recapped what had happened at the hardware store. Robin tucked her phone back into her pocket and waited until Marcus was done with his story before informing them all she had found the group but the only mention of a rental was posted more than two months prior and was surely already taken since there was a list of commentors requesting more information.

Roger asked Jeremiah, "What do you know about Peter Slager? You said you've lived here your entire life."

"I don't know much about him," Jeremiah said. "He moved here about twenty-five years ago. Blew in with the wind, I guess. No one knew him then. Slept in his car at the park until he met his boyfriend. Said he was from Iceland or something. I was a kid back then so I really didn't pay attention, or I was high all the time. I do remember when he started buying houses though. My parents talked about it a lot. Said he was buying up the town to become a slumlord. I think he did it out of spite once he and his boyfriend broke up, if you ask me. Just look at all the houses with lightning rods. At first, there seemed to be a lot surrounding his ex-boyfriend's house, but over time that area grew to what it is now. I've always wanted to get a map of the town and mark all the houses with lightning rods. Some people are convinced there's a pattern or some sort of explanation for the rods. Lots of people have complained about his practices as a landlord but I guess they just end up moving out of town because you don't see them around much after they start complaining. Maybe they realize it's a losing battle. He has so many properties that he just gives people on the town council one whenever he needs things to go his way. He kind of has all the political *and* financial power."

"Ominous." Marcus rubbed his jaw before taking a large drink of his beer and finishing it.

"Shit just keeps getting creepier," Robin said.

Marcus slid his glass toward Roger. "Can I get another? I have a toothache from hell."

Roger nodded, took the glass, and headed toward the tap.

"You should go to a dentist if it's bothering you," Robin said.

"Good luck with that," Jeremiah said. "No one can ever get a hold of the dentist. Everyone seemed to love the guy, but then he stopped answering his phone. His voicemail is full, from what I've heard." He smiled, opened his mouth, and pointed to a few missing teeth in the back of his mouth before shutting it. "Best to just take care of it yourself. Got a set of pliers at home?"

Everyone heard Pan suddenly start making a ruckus outside and Jeremiah excused himself to calm the animal down. Roger returned with Marcus's refreshed pint glass.

Robin said, "You're not pulling your tooth."

Marcus nodded. "I'm sure it'll pass." He rubbed his jaw again before lifting his beer. "This will cure it." He took a large swallow.

Roger said, "I can ask around to see if anyone is renting in town. Tons of townies drink here, or at the bar beside the headshop. You could ask around there. Little Falls is one of those towns where you have to know someone if you need something, from what I gather."

Robin sighed. "You mean we have to make friends."

"Afraid so."

Robin groaned.

"Well," Marcus said, "I guess we'll head there next."

Marcus couldn't help but notice the patron he suspected was listening to their conversation had disappeared.

13

MARCUS AND ROBIN WERE FEELING a pretty good buzz when they left the brewery. It was close to ten PM when they stepped outside. Marcus thought the brewery closed early and could probably make a lot more money if they kept regular bar hours.

They decided it was early enough for the other bar to still be open so they started walking there. It was full dark and the street lights were on but they were few and far between. They were cloaked in darkness.

They were a few blocks from the bar when Robin got an uneasy feeling and looked behind her. A shadow she assumed was a man was following them, trailing about thirty feet behind. Robin swore the stranger made eye contact with her, even though she couldn't be sure in the low lighting. It made her feel uneasy and she quickened her pace, leaving Marcus to lag behind, putting him between her and the stranger.

"Hang on," Marcus said. "What's the hurry? They don't close for two more hours." He walked faster to catch up with her.

When Marcus reached her, she whispered, "Sorry, woman's

instinct. I think we're being followed."

Marcus looked behind him and spotted the shadow of the man. "I think … I think that guy was at the brewery. He's probably going to the bar too since the brewery closes so early." Marcus wanted to run too. He was certain the stranger behind them was the guy listening in on their conversation at the brewery.

The two felt a lot better once they turned onto the street where the bar was located. The lighting was better and there was a small group of people hanging around the door to the bar. The group was talking loudly and smoking cigarettes. Marcus and Robin could clearly hear them shouting about motorcycles and someone they kept referring to as "that dumb cunt." None of the group noticed or cared as the couple excused themselves through the group to reach the door.

Marcus looked back before he entered the bar. The stranger was the man from the brewery. Marcus thought it was odd that he was wearing a coat. Granted, it had cooled down some since the sun had set, but it was still summer.

Marcus opened the door quickly and was met with a blast of '80s music and a group of people were dancing just inside the door. The dancers were packed so tight he wasn't sure he and Robin could make it through to the bar and he didn't want to be standing where he was when the guy following them entered.

Robin shouted, "Fuck this!" She grabbed Marcus's hand and pushed her way through the group.

But there was no pushing their way through. The tightly pressed throng extended through the establishment. The music was super loud and the patrons seemed way too drunk.

"Maybe this wasn't—" Marcus began before Robin clenched his wrist and practically yanked him past the bar, past the pool tables, and out the back door to the patio.

The only difference between the bar and the patio was that it smelled like weed and cigarette smoke and it was outside.

Both of them stopped when they realized why the whole place was so amplified.

Peter. Up on one of the picnic tables, shirtless and dancing, sweaty. People gathered around the picnic table and practically clawed at him like a rock star.

"Jesus fucking Christ," Marcus muttered, knowing the noise would drown him out.

"I can't take this," Robin said. "Let's get the fuck out of here."

On their way out, Marcus yelled into Robin's ear, "Did you notice everyone's shirts!?"

She looked around as they pressed themselves between a couple who looked like they'd escaped from a Phish show's parking lot. The sea of people all wore yellow shirts with the exact same logo printed on the front.

"Are those …?"

Marcus was tired of shouting and didn't say anything until they were outside and away from the smoking crowd.

"Lightning bolts!" he blurted out. "Everyone in there had one!"

They moved in the direction of the state park. Both walking in silence, contemplating what they'd just witnessed and what it meant … other than all those people being Peter's sycophants.

Robin stopped abruptly and clasped her hands to each side of her head like *The Scream* painting. "This is all too fucking much. Tomorrow, we're getting the fuck out of that house. I don't care if we have to live in the U-haul we have to rent."

She lowered her hands and Marcus pulled her in for a hug.

"We'll figure something out," he said.

"Will we?"

He puffed out a sad laugh. "I don't know."

She tensed against him.

"Marcus," she hissed.

"What?"

"Is that the guy who was following us?"

Marcus turned to follow her line of sight. A shadowy figure shambled down the sidewalk toward the bike path.

Marcus, usually extremely passive and not in the least aggressive, said, "I'm going after him."

Robin, usually conflict averse, didn't stop him. Something strange was happening in Little Falls and the only way they were going to get any answers was if they both grew some balls.

She followed him as he stomped toward the shadowy figure.

Once they were far enough from the bar and fully on the bike path, Marcus shouted, "Hey!"

The figure moved a little more quickly before darting off the bike path and into the woods.

Marcus went to the edge of the bike path where they'd lost the figure.

"Hey!" he shouted. "Were you following us? We'd like to talk to you."

Marcus stepped off the bike path and into the woods. He heard a hissing sound.

"Stay away!" the hissing voice said more assertively.

"Who are you?" Marcus said.

Robin moved beside him. Both of them stared into the dark woods. They heard the figure shuffling toward them and Robin thought the person was trying to hide something from them.

As they moved closer, they were able to get a better look at the figure. Definitely a man. Pretty homeless looking. Pungent scent. He might have been the same guy who removed their trash almost as quickly as they could put it on the curb.

"I'm the Renter," he said. "I was the first. I'm always curious about Peter's new acquisitions."

Marcus scoffed. "Acquisitions? What the fuck? We rent from him."

"Yes," the man hissed. "That means he owns you."

"Like hell. We're getting out of here as soon as we can. Probably first thing tomorrow morning."

The man smiled a nearly toothless smile and growled out a laugh. "Hmmm, are you sure you're willing to pay that price?"

"He can take us to court if he wants the remainder of the rent. We're not staying there. And you can't get blood out of a turnip."

"I thought I could … break my lease, as well … once upon a time."

"Why were you following us? Why are you wasting our time?"

"I'm not the only one following you. I'm trying to save you from the consequences of incredibly poor decisions."

"So … what? You used to rent from Peter too? Big deal. It sounds like more than half the town rents from him. I'm sure we're not the only ones to skip town because of that lunatic. As a matter of fact, I'm pretty sure the person who lived in our house skipped town."

"Oh … I still rent from him."

"But you live in the woods or you're homeless or something, right?"

"Oh … it's a home. I live in a seven-foot-deep hole in the ground and pay a thousand dollars a month."

Marcus, still slightly buzzed and growing agitated with how cryptic the man was being, said, "That's absurd. What the fuck is going on here? Why am I listening to you?"

Now the man moved even closer to them. He pulled open the front of his coat. Neither Marcus nor Robin quite knew what they were looking at. It was dark and only a faint light from the bike path penetrated the trees.

"The first time I broke my lease," the man said. "Peter drilled the mailbox into my chest." The man raised the lid of a wall-mount post box with a creak and let it clank back down. "Sad thing is, I never get any mail anymore."

Robin and Marcus were both speechless.

"The second time I broke my lease …" The Renter turned and lowered the back of his jacket and shirt. Angry-looking red nodules covered the guy's dirty back. "… he broke a window and installed it into my flesh."

A smell wafted off the Renter's dirty and infected back and made Robin gag. She grabbed Marcus's hand and said, "Can we go? I think I really need to go."

"Yes," the Renter hissed. "Go back to your house. Go back to your house that isn't yours. You'll be renting forever. At least you're above ground … for now."

With Robin's guidance, Marcus turned and followed her out of the woods.

They were silent the entire way to the tiny house.

14

ROBIN WAS PRETTY SURE MARCUS was still awake. Periodically he'd take a deep breath, but he didn't move or snore, which was pretty common for Marcus. She didn't know how long she'd been lying in bed, staring at the dark ceiling, feeling hopeless and defeated. When they'd arrived home, they'd both climbed the stairs, knocked their heads on the ceiling, Marcus probably said something about a tiny house helmet, and crawled into bed with their clothes on. Neither of them had spoken since talking to the Renter. She was certain Marcus felt the same way she did. She kept trying to come up with an answer to this nightmare and blamed herself for even suggesting they move here.

They were trapped in this rental house forever or … until they died.

The birds had started their morning song, and she thought she could detect the slightest hint of the sky lightening when Marcus finally spoke.

"Do you think we're in a cult?" he whispered.

His voice breaking the pregnant silence startled Robin.

"I don't kn—" she whispered. She thought about all those people wearing those matching yellow shirts. "*They're* in a cult. Not us."

Marcus rolled toward her. "I think we're in a cult now. Peter is never going to let us leave."

"There has to be a way. No one can stop us from getting in your car and driving away."

"You saw what he did to that guy when he tried to break his lease."

They both lay silent, listening to the birds and the town wake up around them.

"What if we left in the middle of the night?" Robin said. "Leave everything and go. That's probably what the people did who lived here before us. That's why all their stuff was still here."

"Do you actually think they left?"

Robin thought about it for a beat. "I hope so. I want to believe so."

Marcus rolled over onto his back and sighed. "I really fucking hate him."

A knock on the window pane startled both of them. The couple tilted their heads back to see Peter staring down at them, grinning like the Cheshire Cat. They'd been baffled by the night's events when they'd crawled into bed and forgotten to cover the window with the curtain.

Furious, Robin sat up and set the curtain in place. The fabric didn't block out Peter's voice.

"Saw you two at the bar last night," Peter said. "Did you like my dancing? I was hoping I'd get to dance with you, Marcus. I bet you're a really good dancer. You guys disappeared though. You missed a good time."

Robin threw her hands up and made an exasperated expression at Marcus, mouthing the words "What the fuck?"

Marcus lay there looking at her wide-eyed. He shrugged and shook his head, mouthing, "I don't know."

Robin bent down and whispered in Marcus's ear. "What do we do?"

"I don't know," he whispered back. "He'll leave eventually. He always does."

They were very still, staring at each other, hoping Peter would leave.

Peter tapped the window. "Heard you two were thinking of

moving. Pretty sure you've already been told, but that's a bad idea. I don't take kindly to people breaking their promise—I mean leases. I put a lot of time and effort into your house and you promised to take care of it. The house has feelings and leaving would break its heart ... and mine."

"Fucking psychopath," Robin whispered.

Marcus nodded.

Peter added, "Don't bother going to the cops. They're the best renters in town. They love the building I set them up in. Oh, and uh, the dance party is the last Saturday of each month. It's customary to attend and bring your next month's rent."

They waited for Peter to continue but he didn't say anything else.

A few minutes passed before Marcus slowly moved the bottom corner of the curtain and peeked out the window. "He's gone."

Robin scuttled over to the edge of the loft and peeked at the ground floor, making sure Peter hadn't let himself in. "I don't see him down there."

"We would've heard the door," Marcus said.

"Would we though? We didn't hear him climb onto the roof. We didn't hear him bring in the new stove."

"True."

"What are we going to do?"

"I don't know."

"I think everyone in town is in on this ... even the police apparently."

"Jeremiah isn't."

"But he lives out past the edge of town. And he was here before Peter." She waited a beat. "And are you sure we can really trust Jeremiah? The Renter said there were other people watching us."

Marcus bit his lip and thought it over. "Roger's a good judge of a person's character. I don't think he'd hang around with someone if he knew they were wrapped up in all this shit."

"Are you sure about that? What about his roommate?"

A scraping noise caught both of their attentions. The sound was coming from outside. They both moved to the tiny window in the loft.

Peter was dragging a huge tarp loaded with large tree logs down the street in front of the house. The pieces of tree were enormous and certainly didn't look like something a single man could drag by himself. The tarp was worn and tattered and the logs rolled off the tarp and into the street as he yanked on it. The wood stopped as if placed strategically in front of the house, blocking their vehicle and the street.

When the tarp was empty Peter looked up at them and waved. He shouted, "You might want to think about paying next month's rent soon!"

The landlord approached Marcus's car, pulling something from his pocket. He squatted and made a stabbing gesture toward one of the tires. The couple could hear the audible hiss as air rushed out of the hole Peter had made.

"Hey!" Marcus yelled. "What the fuck!?"

Peter ignored them and proceeded to the next tire … and the next, until all the tires were flat. Marcus was furious but also afraid he might get stabbed if he ran down to confront the landlord. The couple remained rooted in their spot, staring out the window, as Peter removed their last chance of getting out of Little Falls.

When Peter was done, he turned his attention to the abandoned tarp in the street. He took his time folding the tarp. When he was satisfied with the folding job, he placed the tarp under one arm and started walking down the street, whistling as he went.

Robin's breath hitched and a tear slid down her cheek. "We're fucked."

A movement across the street caught Marcus's attention. He was certain he'd seen a curtain move on the second story of the white, brick house with three front doors across the street. He looked up at the lightning rod on top of the house.

Marcus said, "I think we should try talking to some of the other renters."

Robin wiped her cheek and sniffled. "Are you crazy!? He knows everything! Did you forget about the guy in the woods? That we're being watched? That guy probably told Peter."

Marcus stared at the window curtain across the street he was sure he'd seen move. "I got a feeling we're not the only ones that want to move though. There's no way everyone is on board with this shit."

Marcus's phone vibrated. It was a text from the landlord. It read: SENT ME PHOTO OF YOUR BALLS FOR $50 OFF NEXT MONTH'S RENT.

He showed Robin.

"Screenshot that," she said. "I get sexually harassed online all the time. You never know when it'll come in handy. For blackmail, if nothing else."

Marcus took a screenshot of the text. "Do you think he cares?"

"How many people are following you on your socials?" she asked.

"Quite a bit. I have about 250 followers."

Robin scrunched her face.

"Why? How many do you have?"

"I have like 750 thousand on Instagram alone."

"That seems overwhelming. Why?"

"Start by posting it there. I have a fan who's an attorney. She's been offering anything for a full nude. Maybe I could reach out to her, see if she has any advice."

"Okay. Okay."

Marcus tapped the icon for the one social media app he had on his phone. He was more prone to posting drunk musings than actually using it as a marketing tool for Open Air.

He waited.

And waited.

He tapped the icon for the internet browser.

And waited.

And waited.

He throttled his phone and shook it like it would make any difference.

"What's wrong?" Robin said.

"Do you have internet?"

She turned her screen on and tapped the internet icon.

And waited.

She looked at the bar across the top of her phone.

"Fuck," she said. "I don't even have WiFi or 5G."

"Try texting me," Marcus said.

Robin typed "text" into her phone and sent it to Marcus.

They waited, dread equally dispersed among them.

"I'm not getting anything," he said.

"Motherfucker," Robin snarled. "I'm sure Peter did this somehow."

"How do we work without internet?"

"How do we pay rent without work?"

"Fuck it. Rent is the least of my worries. I'm going to go check the outside of the house."

"Why?"

"I don't know. Maybe there's something … off. Maybe the

psychopath did something."

"I'll make sure everything's hooked up properly in here. I'll also reboot the modem."

"The modem wouldn't keep 5G from working."

Marcus slid out of bed, no need to dress as he was still fully clothed. He stood up, hit his head, said "Fuck my life," and scooted down the stairs. He went out the front door and began making a round of the very scant perimeter of the house, looking for … what, he didn't really know. Cut cords, maybe. Anything out of the ordinary.

He didn't see anything until he got to the north side of the house. A piece of plywood had been pulled away from the foundation. He imagined it was what one would use to access the crawlspace.

"Fuck that," he thought. "I'm not going under there."

He pushed the piece of plywood against the void and held it in place with a nearby stick that was most likely used exactly for this purpose.

He made another round, looking both at the wires running from the road to the front of the house and the wires running from the poles in the alley. Again, he noticed nothing unusual. He wandered out into the middle of the surprisingly large backyard and looked up at the lightning rod. If he squinted, he thought he could see some kind of box toward the top of the lightning rod. He pulled his phone out, zoomed in, and took a photo of it.

Excited to show Robin, he made his way back to the front of the house. A folded piece of paper was taped to the front of the door. He pulled it off and unfolded it.

"Son of a motherfucking bitch," he said.

15

HE OPENED THE DOOR TO find Robin standing naked in the middle of the living room, her camera on the tripod a few feet in front of her. He tossed the piece of paper onto the kitchen table. He was suddenly and inexplicably aroused. Noticing the windows were fully open, he moved behind Robin and got closer.

"Why didn't you draw the blinds?" he said into her ear while putting his hands on her bare hips.

"There aren't any."

He looked at the top of the window frame and wondered when Peter had taken them. "We're going to make him pay." He pressed his hardness against her lower back.

She exhaled softly and said, "This is ... kind of hot."

He moved around to face her and got down on his knees. They continued as if no one was watching even though it was the middle of the day, they were less than twenty feet from the street, and they no longer had any blinds. They finished with Robin bent over the kitchen table, a fistful of her hair in Marcus's hand. When he looked up from her perfect ass and rippling back muscles, he saw Peter watching from his battered car. Marcus was pretty sure he was masturbating and he flashed him the middle finger on both hands. When Robin realized what was happening, she did the same thing.

Peter's car slowly pulled away.

Marcus slowly pulled out.

Robin noticed the piece of paper he'd thrown on the table.

"What's this?" she asked.

"You're not going to like it."

She stayed bent over the table and pulled the paper toward her.

Scrawled across the top was: LEASE EXPLICITLY STATES YOU CANNOT RUN A BUSINESS FROM THIS RENTAL PROPERTY

Below the scrawl was a photocopy of Marcus's business card and Robin's knees from her Bee's Knees page.

In a fit of anger, Robin crumpled up the paper and threw it in the general direction of the trashcan. It missed. Her face went expressionless and cold.

"I'm going to go to the bathroom and clean up," she said.

"I'll start breakfast."

"I'm not hungry."

Marcus had a bowl of oats, quinoa, and hemp milk, staring out the window by the table as he slowly ate, naked. A sweet-smelling breeze came in through the screen. The tall trees on the street shaded everything. Birds sang lazily in the midday sunlight. He took a deep breath. If it weren't for the landlord situation, this would be perfect. He thought about the mold-infested apartment they'd come from. The daily stabbings. The man with suppurating wounds who stayed in his wheelchair in front of the building, smoking cigarettes and harassing people all day. The constant sirens. The heat and air that was always on the fritz and in control of the building manager. The almost daily fire alarm evacuations. The leaky dishwasher. People's disturbed looks when he told them where they lived. He *really* didn't want to go back to that.

Robin seemed more composed when she got out of the shower.

Marcus was standing in front of the door and scratching his balls.

"I guess I should put on some clothes," he said, noticing she was now fully dressed.

"Or don't. It probably doesn't matter anymore."

"We'll figure something out," he said.

She threw her hands up in the air. "I've never felt so fucked before."

"We'll see if Roger's at the brewery tonight. If you want, we can have him take us back to his place. It's not ideal, but he'd understand."

She rubbed her hands against her face. "This is not how I saw my life turning out."

"Me either," he said. "Trust me."

He quickly pulled his clothes back on.

"I need to get out of here," he said. "You want to go for a hike?"

"Might as well. It's not like we can do any work."

They stepped out into the perfect day, trying to forget about the gloom infesting them.

16

ROBIN AND MARCUS MADE THEIR way across town toward the nature reserve. There were no clouds in the sky and they both worked up a sweat before stepping into the canopy of trees. The light breeze rustled the leaves and there didn't seem to be anyone on the trails, which Marcus attributed to it being the middle of a weekday.

They made their way down the entrance path. It ended at a cross path that ran along the edge of a cliff. They stood at the T, contemplating which way they should go.

Robin noticed that across from them a "#1" was written on a piece of laminated paper and stapled to a leaning post set in the ground. Under the first sign was a chunk of flat wood with the words "STAY ON THE TRAILS" sloppily hand-carved into it. Barely noticeable, someone had written in marker on the wood sign: "EAT SHIT CUNT" and had drawn a pentagram below their message. Weather and time had worn all the messages.

The combination of the hand-carved sign and the lack of any barrier between the trail and the cliff made Robin break out in gooseflesh. It wasn't the marker message that chilled her, but the carved letters of the wood sign, as if someone had done it in a hurry. She looked to Marcus, who was still contemplating which way they should go.

"I don't think it matters which way we go as long as we stay on the path." She pointed at the sign.

Marcus squinted as he read the sign and laughed at the marker wielder's message. "Guess someone's not a rule follower."

"I think we should go left," she said. "It's sloped down. I'd prefer the fall to be short if I go over the cliff."

"Makes sense."

The couple started down the path, Robin in the lead as Marcus wanted to be able to catch her if she did slip. The first part of the trail was rocky and made them both nervous as neither of them had the appropriate shoes. The pitch of the trail grew steeper as they went and Marcus was the one who made a misstep. His foot slid in the dirt and he caught himself before landing on his arse. Luckily, they were near the landing of flat ground and another division in the path.

"Holy fuck!" Robin shouted out of fear. "Are you hurt?"

"Just my pride." He righted himself and hurried down to the flat area.

Robin looked back and forth at the divided trail. She'd always had a solid sense of direction. "That way would head toward town." She pointed to the left.

"I can't tell if it's the leaves rustling, but it sounds like there's water this way." He thumbed toward the right.

Robin noticed the pitch of the right-hand trail descended also. She was sure to be cautious as she took the lead again. The path was rockier than the first and disappeared around a copse of trees. Right before they reached the bend a man rounded the corner with a large black dog off its leash. The couple hugged the right side of the trail to pass the man and his pet. The canine stopped in its tracks and began to growl at them. Robin and Marcus froze. The owner didn't seem to care about his dog terrorizing them.

The man sighed heavily. "Oh, shut up, Satan."

Marcus noticed the dog's fur rise between its shoulder blades. "Um, could you hold him while we pass?"

"For fuck's sake," the man murmured under his breath. He snatched the dog's collar, which was nearly invisible as it was the same color as the animal's coat. He yanked on the collar, trying to drag the animal up the hill, but the dog wouldn't budge. It continued to growl and snarl, baring its teeth. "Come on, Satan, move yer fuckin' ass!" Still, the dog stood rooted. "Jus' go around!" he shouted at the couple.

Robin's heart hammered. She was normally a little scared of dogs in general, but she felt like she was on the verge of crying and pissing her pants simultaneously. Marcus put himself between the beast and Robin and guided her down and past it. She couldn't take her eyes off the creature as Marcus guided her. She tripped and stumbled into him. They were less than a foot from the dog as they passed it and she wasn't confident the man would be able to control it as the animal probably weighed as much as him.

The dog lunged at them once they were past it, knocking its owner to the ground. Fortunately, the man had a death grip on the collar as the canine snarled and desperately tried to jump in Robin and Marcus's direction.

"Goddamn it! Ya stupid fuckin' mutt!" the man yelled while lying on the ground.

The couple hightailed it around the corner where the path leveled out. They discovered a sturdy wooden bridge over a robust stream. As they took the few steps up to the wooden structure, they heard a dog's yelp from the direction they'd come from.

Robin was shaking and breathing rapidly. Marcus took her hand and they ran across the bridge, too terrified to stop and enjoy the beauty of nature. On the other side of the bridge was a small waterfall and pool. They slowed as they descended the bridge's steps. The waterfall had dampened the stairs and made them slick.

Marcus looked back down the empty bridge. "I don't think it's coming after us."

"Thank everything that is unholy." Robin flopped down on a large rock by the pool at the end of the pint-size waterfall. She put her hands on her knees and tried to steady her breathing.

"Are you okay?" Marcus asked.

"Yeah, I think I just need a minute." She dipped down, scooped up a handful of the cool water, and splashed it on her neck. She sipped a handful of the water and it tasted like it was thick with iron.

Marcus noticed the path divided again. He fished his phone out of his back pocket, looked at it, cursed, and put it back in his pocket.

"Still no signal?"

"Nope. I was hoping I could find a map of these trails online. I'm never gonna remember how to get back."

Robin tapped her temple. "I'm good at memorizing landmarks." After a few minutes she stood and looked down both paths. She chose the level one, opposite the side with an incline.

Marcus took the lead this time, in case they ran into another situation. They came across a boardwalk built barely above the surface of a swampy area. They could hear the multiple calls of some sort of frog they couldn't see and it sounded more like the pluck of a spring. *Bong bong bong.* Robin started at the sound of a large splash nearby. She wasn't sure what it was but a lurking fear something was making its way toward them under the layer of green slime floating on the water made her paranoid. She was happy when they made it back onto dry ground, again finding themselves at a divided path: one continuing over the swamp, the other up a small hill where they could hear voices. They chose the hill.

At the top of the hill, they found a shaded clearing and a calm, shallow, and wide stream. A couple was seated at the water's edge, their naked feet in the water, watching a child walk around in the stream, picking rocks out of the riverbed under a sign that read: STAY OUT OF THE WATER.

The couple acknowledged their presence but said nothing. Marcus looked around and Robin approached the stream.

Robin noted the water was clear. Someone had taken the time to place large stones at equal intervals to create a makeshift path across the stream. She saw a part in the tall grass on the other side. It didn't look like an official trail. Probably something some local teenagers made to hide and make out or smoke weed.

Marcus approached Robin and said, "Looks like we have two options. Climb the rocky hill …" He pointed to the hill where a post was stuck in the ground with another laminated sign, this time with a "#4" stapled to it. "Or along the stream." He pointed in the opposite direction at a narrow path against the water's edge.

"I'm tired of hills," she said. "There's also this." Robin pointed at the rock path across the stream.

Marcus scrutinized the narrow part in the grass on the other side. "Is that a real path?"

Robin shrugged.

Marcus looked back at the other options and spotted the other couple giving him the stink eye. "Okay, let's try it."

"We can always backtrack."

"True."

They made their way across the stream, one stone at a time, with Robin in the lead. Once they were on the other side they discovered the path was very narrow and the vegetation was overgrown.

"I'm not sure this is a path," Marcus said.

"Someone made it for a reason. The stone bridge alone had to have taken a few people to build. I don't think I could lift one of those by myself."

After a few minutes of walking, the grass became less dense and shorter in the shadows of the trees. It was knee high and tickled Robin's knees. She stopped to take a photo of her knees surrounded by all the greenery, an overwhelming surge of hopelessness flickering through her. She didn't know if anyone would ever see it if she wasn't allowed to run her business from home.

Marcus noted the path was now no wider than the width of someone's foot. "This trail is definitely not a regular path. I'm not sure if we should go much farther. I feel like we're going to get lost, and we don't have any way to call for help since my phone can't get a signal."

"I'm sure it's something some kids made that leads to a party spot. Let's see where it goes and then we'll double back. I swear, we won't get lost."

They continued on for another ten minutes. As Marcus was about to suggest they give up and double back, he spotted something.

"Wait," he said. "What's that?"

They both stopped and looked ahead. Not far from where they were stood a dark-colored house ... and jutting up through the trees was the largest lightning rod either of them had ever seen.

17

"DO YOU THINK …?" MARCUS SAID.

Robin, overcome with a choking fear, struggled to say, "I … I think it has to be. Right? I mean . . . who else could it be?"

Marcus continued staring at the modest two-story house. It looked like it had grown up from the forest floor, covered in moss and ivy, almost indiscernible from the ground below it.

Robin fought for breath. She felt like they were being watched.

"I feel like we should do something," Marcus said.

Robin swallowed, a dry click issuing from her throat. "We don't *have* anything."

"I feel like we should at least do something to let him know we were here, that we know where he lives."

"I don't know …" Robin said.

Marcus sensed her hesitation.

"Fine," he said. "You stay here. I'll do it."

"What are you gonna do?"

Marcus looked around at the ground. Finding a softball-sized rock, he bent, picked it up, and said, "I'm gonna break a fucking window."

Robin sucked in a breath. Marcus knew this was her way of saying she didn't think it was a good idea.

"How's he going to know it was us?" he said.

"What if he's in there? What if he's watching?"

Marcus tossed the rock back and forth between each hand.

"You know what? I don't care. I get the feeling no one here is doing anything to fight back."

"Well ... vandalism's illegal. You could get in trouble."

"The way I see it, it isn't *vandalism*. It's self-defense. He took our window blinds. *He's* the one vandalizing *our* house."

"Except he owns it, so it's *his* house. Maybe we could just get a lawyer or something. There has to be a better way out of this."

Marcus uttered a strange-sounding laugh. "There *might* be, but you know what? I want to do it. Right now, just the thought of throwing a rock through that fucker's window is the first happy thought I've had in a while."

"Okay," Robin said. "I'm going to stay here. I'd rather be an accessory than an accomplice."

"Fine," Marcus said. "You can be my lookout."

Whatever semblance of a trail ended where they stood. Marcus took a deep breath, girding himself, and began stalking toward the house. Robin stood exactly where she was, aware of the tension in her body, her hands clutched into fists at her sides. She wondered what Marcus would do if Peter saw him and came out of the house to stop him. Would he actually fight back? Dear god, would he throw the rock at him? Was Marcus really that mad?

Then she felt a bit of what she heard in Marcus's laugh. Bloodlust. Or something like it. If Peter tried to stop him and Marcus smashed him over the head with a rock, she'd cheer. She'd feel triumphant. Astoundingly, she realized it was something she wanted to happen. She really hoped that creepy piece of shit would walk out the front door.

Marcus came to an abrupt stop about twenty feet from the house.

She continued staring at him and noticed his stopping wasn't voluntary.

He turned to her and called, "I'm stuck!"

She began walking toward him and noticed the ground getting softer, like the swampy area they'd walked through earlier except

THE LANDLORD

there was no water on the surface. The ground was just sludge. She stopped, not wanting to get stuck.

Not to be dissuaded by the mucky terrain, Marcus brought the rock back and let it fly. It thudded harmlessly on the porch, sitting there like a dud.

Rustling and human yelps came from the distance. Robin spun in a circle, looking for the source.

Marcus, a little closer than she was, must have seen something she couldn't. He turned back to her and yelled, "Run!"

Before she turned to commit herself to a sprint straight back to the house, she saw him desperately trying to heave himself from the soft earth. Then, almost against her will, she trained her vision on the almost non-existent trail and ran as fast as she could.

18

ROBIN DIDN'T STOP RUNNING UNTIL she reached the Little Falls toward the opening of the reserve. There were a few groups of people waiting their turn to get their pictures taken with it, and she finally felt like she wouldn't be scooped up by whoever she'd heard in the woods.

A barefoot guy with a Grateful Dead shirt watched her draw to a stop and struggle to catch her breath.

"Hey?" he said. "Everything okay?"

Her mouth was dry and she struggled to produce enough saliva to say something. She wanted to tell him that everything was not okay but she could barely say anything. The only thing she could think to do was to keep walking.

"Do you think she's okay?" she heard the man say to the dread-locked woman he'd been standing with.

"She's probably fine," the woman said. "Maybe she's a trail runner or something."

Even though she'd slowed to a walk, Robin's heart still raced and she struggled to take a full breath. When she finally got out of the reserve, she gave herself a moment to stop and quiver with rage and fear. She also wanted to give herself a minute to make sure Marcus wasn't right behind her. Maybe he'd managed to extricate himself from the swampy soil. Maybe that wasn't a band of Peter loyalists she'd heard in the woods. Maybe it was a group of hikers that could've freed Marcus.

Once she convinced herself Marcus wasn't going to come out of the reserve any time soon, she began walking back to the tiny house, slowly, because she had no real desire to be there either. She passed several groups of people out walking. She didn't recognize any of them. She realized she saw the people around town differently now. At first, everyone had seemed so friendly and welcoming. Now she saw that as an act. They were the honey to Peter's bitter medicine. She and Marcus had done their best to smile and nod at people as they walked past, even though neither one of them was really that type of person. She couldn't help but look at people with a deep sense of suspicion.

She turned onto the end of their street and her stomach sank as she saw Peter's car parked on the street, the logs prohibiting him from getting an actual parking spot. He had his trailer hooked up to the back of the vehicle and she heard banging and grunting before she even came up on the house.

She didn't see him right away. The sounds were coming from the back of the house. Without Marcus, part of her was terrified to be around Peter. But there was another part of her that was furious. For the first time in her life she wished she carried a knife or a gun or something, even though she knew she'd probably just end up injuring herself if she had either of those things.

She took a deep breath and tried to calm her nerves before entering the yard and walking toward the back of the house.

Peter was back there, shirtless and glistening and ... removing one of the walls from the house?

"What the hell is this?" she said, not even entertaining the idea of being nice.

He dropped his hammer and turned to her.

He didn't look angry. She was assuming the wall removal was punishment for something, probably the working-from-home thing, but he didn't look upset about anything.

He smiled, the look in his eyes completely insane.

"I get the feeling you two aren't happy here. I started thinking about why and figured it must be because of the size of the place. By the way you've been acting, it's obvious you're having some difficulty with living in such a small place. So I've decided to … open it up a bit."

"By removing the fucking wall?"

"By *expanding* the house. I'm not even going to enforce a rent increase."

"So when's it going to be finished?" She didn't even know why she was entertaining this lunatic.

He wiped sweat from his brow and bent to pick up his hammer. Instinctively, Robin flinched.

"I should have this wall removed by the end of the day. As for when the project'll be completed … well, that depends. With these tariffs and inflation and everything, the cost of lumber's a little high right now. But I'm looking, maybe I'll find something I can repurpose." He took a gloating breath as he pulled his lips back into that punch-worthy smile. "But … I won't know until that happens."

"So what are we …?" She threw her hands out in a form of exhausted surrender. "You know what? Fuck it. Make sure you're out of here by dark."

He chuffed out an irritating laugh.

"I don't really have a choice. Yeah, I think I must've cut the power at some point so, well, I'll have to look into that too."

Robin rolled her eyes before turning away from him and heading … where? She had no idea. Her legs felt like jelly. She couldn't think about anything other than being terrified for Marcus's safety and her unbridled rage toward Peter. She went in the direction of the brewery.

She stopped.

She had a thought.

They couldn't leave the town by car because he'd slashed their tires and placed logs in the road that no one from the city had bothered removing.

But what if she simply walked out?

She had no doubt that if she could leave the confines of Little Falls, her phone would magically have a signal again, and she could call an Uber or something to take her to a hotel or somewhere safe. She could hire someone to go retrieve Marcus.

She took a deep breath, the sliver of hope temporarily overshadowing her exhaustion. After all, she was less than a mile from the town's border. She could be there in less than fifteen minutes.

She made it to the end of Hafford and turned onto Main St., which would take her out of town. She noticed a line of cars heading out of town and her hope rapidly diminished. She had a suspicion that was quickly affirmed after walking only a hundred feet or so. The road to and from town was blocked by a large tree.

"I'm on foot," she thought. "I'll simply walk around."

As she drew closer, she began to realize how massive the tree was, covering the entirety of the road and into a ditch on either side. She was prepared to get messy. She walked around the trunk-side of the tree. She assumed if it had come down during the storm, that it would have been removed by now. Unsurprisingly, when she looked at the trunk, she noticed the tree had not been struck by lightning or simply fallen down. The cut was smooth. Someone had cut the tree down with a chainsaw.

How was anyone in the town okay with this?

She walked around, a shocking and sudden feeling of elation washing over her. She came up from the drainage ditch and onto the road. She felt like running and skipping as she walked toward what she could only think of as freedom. She decided she was going to keep walking until she saw a car. Maybe she would inform them they wouldn't be able to get into town because of the tree and politely ask if they could give her a ride somewhere.

She walked for what felt like a mile. Not a single car approached. Granted, it had been a few weeks since they'd been on this road, but she was no longer sure it was even the same road. Normally, she trusted her instincts when it came to landmarks and directions, but none of this felt familiar.

Finally she saw someone.

A man walking a goat.

Jeremiah.

She didn't call out or stop him. She found herself actually slowing down so she didn't draw his attention. She thought about turning around but felt too invested in the time she'd already spent walking.

Once again, her hopes were dashed when she saw the sign for the Dollar General in front of her.

The road had taken her around the perimeter of the town.

She entered the town from the other side, and a deep sense of dread filled her. What had maybe only been annoyance previously now darkened into outright fear.

She continued toward the brewery on legs that were tired of moving. She hoped Roger would be there because she thought what she needed now more than anything was a familiar face.

19

ROBIN COULDN'T STOP THINKING ABOUT Marcus still back in the woods as she made her way to the brewery. She tried very hard not to think about the road out of town. Before they could even entertain the thought of leaving, she now knew they would have to take care of the landlord problem. Since Peter had been destroying the house when she made it back home, she could only assume Marcus was still stuck in the muck at the house in the woods. There was no way Peter could be in two places at the same time. She wasn't sure why Marcus told her to run. She felt guilty as hell leaving him behind.

The worry ate at her. She felt her stomach roll and bent forward just in time to vomit in someone's front yard, all over a patch of lovely flowers being pollinated by a couple of fat, lazy bumblebees. The bees acted indignant for a moment and finally flew off. Robin spat a few times. There seemed to be a bit of food clinging to the back of her tongue, except ... it felt like it was moving. She hacked and spat and ran a finger across her tongue, digging at whatever was back there. She finally managed to dislodge it and pulled her finger from her mouth. A worm, no longer than a dime's width, wriggled on her finger.

The world spun around her and she tried weakly to scream before the world went black.

~

Robin woke in a dark and cool room. The drapes were drawn shut. The scant light peeking through the crack in the middle of the curtains told her the sun was either rising or setting. She couldn't be sure which and instinctively reached for her phone in her back pocket. Panic. She realized she didn't have pants on, and the garment she wore felt too large for her. Everything that had happened came flooding back and she threw the covers off and left the bed, stumbling around in the darkened room, feeling the walls until she found a light switch.

The overhead light was bright and a sickly yellow. It took a few seconds for her eyes to adjust to the light as she scanned the room. The furniture was old but well taken care of. Makeup, fake nails, and false eyelashes covered the top of a dresser and a vanity. Large, teased wigs were hung on a wooden coat rack. And clothes were bulging out of the closet that was missing a door. She caught her reflection in a full-length mirror. Someone had changed her clothes and she now wore an oversized Lady Gaga shirt.

Faintly, she could hear a television playing somewhere in the house. A familiar, upbeat jingle she couldn't quite place. *An older sitcom?* she thought, trying to remember what the show was called. She also heard the sound of a dryer running nearby.

She went to the window and peeked through the curtains. Large overgrown bushes obscured her view but she could see there was another house on the other side of the vegetation. Knowing there was another house that close set her mind at ease a little. She didn't think someone who wanted to harm her would put her within screaming distance of other people.

Robin approached the door, placed her hand on the knob, and cut the light. She waited a beat for her eyes to readjust to the darkness and then began to slowly turn the doorknob, trying not to make any noise. She just wanted to find her clothes and get to the brewery. She needed to find Marcus but she was going to need Roger's help.

She opened the door into a darkened hallway. Across from her was a bathroom. The light was on and she could tell that was where the dryer sounds were coming from. A few more doors were located down the hall and at the end she saw the flickering light of a television illuminating what she could only assume was the living room. She saw an empty rocking chair with an old afghan draped over it.

She quietly crossed the hall to the bathroom and shut the door with a quiet click, which sounded like a shotgun blast to Robin. She hoped whoever was watching television hadn't heard her. The bathroom walls were covered in worn wallpaper adorned with garish purple flowers. The cloth shower curtain was lavender and had ruffles around the edges.

Robin's bladder was full and ached. She relieved herself before washing her hands with a perfume-smelling bar of soap sitting on the sink's edge. She splashed water on her face and rinsed her mouth, which she thought tasted like vomit.

She remembered vomiting into someone's flowers, then she remembered the worm and almost gagged. A flower-printed hand towel hung beside the sink but Robin used the shirt she was wearing to dry her face. She contemplated opening the dryer and searching for her clothes, but the timer said it still had an hour left and she was sure stopping the dryer would alert whoever was in the living room. When she was done washing up, she left the bathroom and headed toward the sound of the television at the end of the hall. She heard the laugh track of the TV show, accompanied by two different laughs from within the room.

Robin stepped into a semi-darkened living room. The television was playing an episode of *The Golden Girls*. A small lamp put off weak light on an end table nestled between a recliner and a sofa. An elderly woman with large glasses in a dressing gown and slippers was reclined in the recliner. A broad-shouldered, middle-aged woman in a dress with big hair and a perfectly painted face sat on the sofa, her legs crossed and her hands folded over one knee. Robin could tell the woman on the sofa was tall even though she was sitting.

"There she is," the elderly woman said.

The woman on the sofa looked at her. In an obvious falsetto voice she said, "Your clothes are in the dryer, but they might still be pretty damp."

It dawned on Robin that the woman on the sofa was most likely born male.

The elderly woman pushed a button on the arm of the recliner, activating a motor within the chair to retract the footrest and set the recliner into a position so the woman could stand up. "Jackie found ya layin' in the flower bed by the sidewalk and brought ya in. You were covered in yer own sick. Figured ya wouldn't mind if a couple of broads cleaned ya up."

The woman on the sofa waved her hand slightly at Robin when the elderly woman said the name Jackie.

"Uh," Robin said. "No. I guess I don't mind."

"Name's Mattie Blitch," the old woman said, shuffling toward a lit kitchen beyond the living room. "You want something to eat or drink?"

Jackie stood. Robin was correct in her assessment. Jackie was a foot taller than her, not including the hair, which added at least another six inches. Jackie waved her hand to insinuate that Robin lead the walk to the kitchen.

"Uh, sure," Robin said, walking into the kitchen.

Rooster photos and trinkets lined the walls of the small kitchen. A red, Formica-top table sat in the middle of the room.

"Have a seat," Jackie said. "What's yer name, hun?" She took a seat across from Robin.

"Robin. Robin Gray."

Mattie pulled a container from the fridge and popped the lid open before placing it in the microwave and turning it on.

Robin found it odd that the old woman assumed she wanted whatever was in that container without asking her. But Robin didn't really care. She was ravenous. And thirsty.

"Can I get some water," Robin said.

"Hope ya don't mind tap," Jackie said.

Robin shook her head. She'd drunk water out of the waterfall and ended up with a worm in her stomach. The tap water couldn't be that bad. She tried to remember the last time she'd had a tetanus shot, then decided it really didn't matter and wouldn't work if she was filled with parasites.

Jackie stood to get her water while Mattie rummaged around in the silverware drawer and retrieved a fork. The microwave dinged and it wasn't long before Robin was chugging a glass of water and scarfing down a container of lukewarm spaghetti while the two women watched her silently with questioning eyes.

Robin finished the pasta and Mattie gave her an approving wink.

"I'm gonna go catch the end of my show," she said, slowly and painfully making her way back into the living room.

"At least you have an appetite," Jackie said. "I, for one, have eaten so much of Mattie's award-winning spaghetti I don't even think I taste it anymore."

"Award-winning." Robin didn't know what else to say. "That's impressive."

"Shhh," Jackie said. "I gave her the award. It would break her heart if she knew it wasn't real." Jackie looked toward a sheet of paper fastened to the refrigerator with a magnet. It looked like the kind of award certificate you printed from your computer and gave to kindergarten students. "Of course, if I'd known it would lead to her making two batches a week, I probably never would have done it."

While Robin was thoroughly interested in the spaghetti drama, she knew there were other things she needed to do. She needed to find Marcus. She needed to tell Roger. She needed to get out of Little Falls. But how? Their car was immobile. Leaving on foot was apparently impossible. She guessed they could try being airlifted but doubted they had the resources for that. She felt lost and overwhelmed, and whenever she got overwhelmed she just shut down. Her flight or fight response was set to opossum.

"How are you feeling?" Jackie asked.

Something inside Robin broke. Of course she and Marcus loved each other, but they'd both become embroiled in the landlord fiasco, and therefore sometimes unaware of the other's feelings. The landlord and everything that had happened to them since moving here had seemed unbelievably uncaring and cruel. The tears came and she had trouble forming words.

Jackie wrapped a big hand around one of Robin's considerably smaller ones and said, "Take your time. Tell me when you're ready. We all go through shit sometimes. Literally. This morning as I was having my first cigarette of the day, I had such a bad coughing fit I almost shit my pants. Maybe it means I need to stop."

Robin couldn't help but laugh a little through the tears.

"It's ... a lot," Robin said.

"Well ... I've got time. Tell me about it."

Robin wanted to talk about it but felt like she was abandoning Marcus the longer she talked. Shouldn't she be trying to help him? Then she had to ask herself what she could possibly do. Go back into the woods and wrest Marcus away from a group of impassioned, semi-feral Peter followers?

"I don't know what's going on," she said. "We have this landlord and, holy shit, he's making our lives a living hell."

Jackie closed her eyes and nodded her head in sympathy. "You must mean Peter Slager."

"You know who I'm talking about?"

"There probably isn't a person in this town who wouldn't know who you're talking about. Almost everyone here has had to deal with him at some point or the other. He's a nuisance to practically everyone. He practically owns all of Little Falls."

"Why is that?" Robin asked.

"You mind coming out to the porch with me?" Jackie grinned. "I've decided to start smoking again. Don't worry. I'll try my damnedest to not shit my pants."

Robin returned the smile and said, "Okay." She liked this person. It was odd. She made her feel safe and lightened the whole oppressive mood surrounding her, even though she knew she should be in straight-up panic mode.

Jackie grabbed a pouch of American Spirit tobacco from the top of the microwave and Robin followed her through the living room and out the back door. The porch light was bright and Robin realized it must be late as the sun had set. The backyard was wildly overgrown, huge trees making it feel like they'd stepped out of a wooded cottage and not a house in the middle of a modern-day village. Insects sang in the night around them.

"I really need to get somebody out here to do something about this," Jackie said, looking around at the overgrown yard.

"I kind of like it," Robin said. "It's like a living privacy fence."

Jackie plopped down in an old lawn chair, retrieved a citronella candle on the ground beside her chair, lit it, and returned it to its spot. Robin sat in the chair beside her.

"That's what I keep telling Mattie. She wants the place to look like a zen garden and I keep telling her that manicured stuff is boring and sterile."

"Are you two … roommates?"

"I'd like to think we are at this point. I started as her home health aide after her wife died. We got along famously and the agency didn't pay me for shit anyway. Only reason I did it was so I'd have my evenings free to do drag shows around the state. That's my true livelihood, but it's a pretty unreliable income. Mattie told me I could move in and keep doing what I'd been doing with the agency and she wouldn't charge me rent or anything. It was too good to pass up. She's like a big sister I never had. A real old big sister."

"Not a mother?"

"Nah. I already had a mother and she was the biggest cunt I knew. Mattie's nice. Mattie accepts me for who I am and always has."

Jackie dexterously rolled a cigarette and offered it to Robin, who shook her head. She lit up, her face brightening and her posture relaxing.

"So where were we?" she said.

"Peter, the landlord."

"*Riiiight.*" Jackie drew the word out as she exhaled smoke.

"So how do you know him?"

"Like I said before—if you live here, you at least know of him. I haven't really had much interaction with him, but apparently after Mattie's wife died, he wanted to buy her out of this place. It's like the man wants to own everybody's house. He did some real KKK intimidation-type shit. He burnt her pride flags. He'd throw bags of shit onto her porch. Send letters. Leave intimidating messages. Mattie's a tough old thing and she wasn't having any of it. It also helps that she's on pretty good terms with Deputy Penny, who might be one of the only non-corrupt members of the Little Falls police department."

"Yeesh. Maybe we need to get in touch with her."

"Them. Penny's non-binary."

"Cool."

"Yeah? I don't have to explain to you what that is?"

"I'm not ancient. I'm also not a bigot."

Jackie took another drag and said, "I think we'll get along just fine."

"So … why do you think he wants to buy all the houses in town? What's the end game? I can't believe he still has renters."

"It's something Mattie and I have talked about. Nothing's concrete. She doesn't really get out much and most of her old friends are dead. I only really hang out with the fags and queers and weirdos in town and I've even seen a few of them cross over to the dark side."

"We were at a bar the other night and he had quite the crowd. It was a musical performance … or an open mic, I guess, but it almost felt like a rally."

"This is where our theory arises. I did a bit of research on him a few years ago. There really wasn't a lot out there. I'm sure you probably have to give him paper checks or something, right? Dude is famously not online. Still carries the flip phone?"

Robin nodded.

"The only thing I could find was that he'd been a teacher in a neighboring city for a while. But there's where it ends. Starting a decade ago, there's absolutely no information about him. Not even so much as a mention in the local paper. So how does a former public-school teacher have the funds to buy up the majority of the houses in the area? Those people you saw at the show are his 'renters,' but they're really just scattered in tents and bunkers throughout the woods. I think he likes to lure in as many people as he can. Makes him look more important than he really is. And if they think he has the power to make their lives better or worse, they'll fall in line right behind him."

"Strength in numbers."

"Exactly. This town was started as a hippie commune long before there were hippies. Around the sixties, it became a tourist attraction when hippiedom became a sellable commodity. They had the head shops and the metaphysical bookstores and the nature reserves and an extremely liberal arts college."

"Still do."

"Exactly. But tourism is our main industry. Imagine what it would look like if the people coming here knew it was all basically a front and that one guy owns almost everything? And his values absolutely do not align with what people think of Little Falls. Love. Peace. Free thinkers."

"So he's ..."

"He's something. He's here to acquire as much property as possible. He wants to own the entire town. He's probably seventy-five percent there. The other twenty-five percent ... well, that's just a matter of time since most of them are senior citizens. They're the stronghold. The old hippies. Socialism is their game and you'll have to rip it from their cold, dead hands."

"How does he get away with it?"

"When you're rich, you can get away with anything, hun."

"But why can't we just leave? I'm pretty sure he won't let us leave. I tried walking out before I came here and ... it was just a loop. I ended up walking back in the other side of town."

"The goal is to wear you down until this seems normal. The goal is for you to stick around because ..."

"Strength in numbers. Fuck. I don't want this to ever be normal."

Jackie crushed out her cigarette in an empty ashtray.

"Want me to give Deputy Penny a call?"

THE LANDLORD

Robin felt like she was being a serious imposition to Jackie and Mattie, but she wanted answers. More than anything, she wanted to make sure Marcus was okay. If Jackie were to contact Deputy Penny, maybe they could go out there and locate him, make sure he was okay. "I would be eternally grateful," Robin said.

20

THEY RETREATED BACK INTO THE house after Jackie made the call. Jackie made her way back to the sofa and Robin spotted her phone on an end table. Jackie unhooked the cell phone from a charging cord and handed it to Robin.

Robin thumbed the screen, trying to wake the phone. The screen stayed dark. She hit the power button on the side. Nothing. "Huh," Robin said. She stared at the dead phone's screen.

"What's the matter?" Mattie said, reclined and enjoying her show.

"My phone's dead."

"It's been charging for a couple hours now," Jackie said.

"It wasn't getting a signal anyway. It just stopped working. Marcus's phone too."

"It's them damn lightnin' rods, I tell ya!" Mattie shouted. "You got one of those where ya live?"

"Yes."

"Ewww, that greasy bastard Peter. Ain't nobody's house safe with him around. That idiot climbin' up on the houses and messin' with all those rods, thinkin' he's a scientist or somethin'. I hope he falls and breaks his neck one of these days. Fuckin' Nazi."

"Now, Mattie," Jackie said, "don't get your blood pressure up about Peter again. You know what the doctor said about that. It isn't worth it."

Mattie huffed and shook her head disapprovingly before turning her attention back to the television. She grumbled something, but Robin nor Jackie could understand what she said, and then laughed along with the laugh track on TV.

"Your clothes *might* be dry by now," Jackie said. "No guarantees. The dryer is older than Mattie, I swear."

"I'll check," Robin said. "Might be nice to have some pants on before the Deputy arrives."

Robin headed toward the bathroom. The dryer was still running and she pulled the door open to stop it. She was blasted with hot, moist air. Her shirt was dry, but her shorts' pockets still felt damp. They'd have to do. She heard a new voice coming from the living room as she finished dressing and tossed the Lady Gaga shirt in the dirty clothes hamper before exiting the bathroom.

Robin entered the living room to find that Deputy Penny had arrived. The Deputy was tall and imposing. Their hair was pulled back into small space buns and their nails were painted a Tiffany blue. Sitting beside the deputy was a brown, Royal poodle wearing a black vest with "K9 UNIT" embroidered on it.

Introductions were made and Deputy Penny concluded by asking, "So what seems to be the problem?"

Robin felt a lot calmer now and was able to relay her afternoon with what she thought was enough reliability to be accurate. But the more she described the events, the more unsure of herself she seemed.

Penny had scrawled some notes while Robin spoke and now looked at their little pad like they could find the answers somewhere in it.

"Do you think he's in immediate danger?" they said.

"That's the thing," Robin said. "I guess it depends on what you mean by 'danger.'"

"Physical harm."

Robin had to think. At this point, Peter had pretty much demolished their livelihoods and seemed to be in a slow process of destroying their house ... but he had yet to lay a finger on either one of them or even threaten them in any way.

"It's hard to say," Robin said. "I mean … if he's being prevented from leaving that's … physical harm in some way, isn't it? He could be restrained."

"Good Christ!" Mattie blurted. "The girl's worried, Pen! Take her out there and have a look. It's not like you have anything else to do but sit around in your car and talk to Conkles like she even knows what you're sayin'. Maybe you miss out on stoppin' someone goin' thirty in a twenty-five zone. I think the town'll be okay."

"It's getting late," Penny said. "There won't be any rangers on duty right now. Do you think you can find this place again in the dark?"

Robin thought about it. The state park was pretty large. Thankfully it wasn't her that got abducted or whatever. Marcus would never be able to remember where she was. However, they'd walked a long distance, and she'd run most of the way back. In short, she was exhausted. The adrenaline had worn off and her legs felt rubbery and weak. But she needed to find Marcus.

"I think I can find it," Robin said.

"And you've tried calling his phone?" Penny said.

"I can't. My phone's dead."

"And it ain't waking up," Jackie chimed in.

"You try using someone else's phone?" Penny said.

Robin felt embarrassed. "I … don't actually know Marcus's number."

Penny thought about this a second. "I guess I don't really know anybody's number either." They went back to looking at their notepad, this time tapping it with a painted nail, still trying to find a way to not have to work too hard. "Okay. But first, let's go by your house just to make sure he's not there. He might've gotten free and I assume home would be the first place he'd go."

"I'm not so sure about that, but let's check it out anyway," Robin said.

Penny waved at the others in the room and said, "Ladies. Always good seeing you."

Robin thanked them ferociously for their hospitality.

"Feel free to come back anytime," Jackie said. "And now we know where to find you."

"You're welcome anytime," Robin said. She didn't want to sound too rushed but she really wanted to find Marcus.

Robin followed Penny out to their Bronco. It was rusted out and white with TFPD spray-painted on the door. It looked like something a slob would drive.

"Budget's a little tight," Penny said.

Robin again thought about how much she liked this town and how perfect it would be if it didn't contain Peter.

Penny opened the back door and Conkles hopped up into the floorboard and then onto the seat, her tail thumping the cushion and her tongue sticking out of her mouth, blissfully unaware.

Penny rubbed Conkles' head and said, "She's real happy right now. She likes to have a sense of purpose. If your boyfriend's out there, she'll find him. She's a good tracker."

Penny shut the door and headed around to the driver's side. Robin opened the passenger-side door, it squeaked loudly in the night, and climbed in.

Penny started the engine and grabbed a pack of Kentucky's Best cigarettes. Their window was already down. They lit the cigarette and took a deep drag.

"I'm warning you," she said. "I got COPD and I'm not the greatest hiker, so this might not be the quickest operation."

"Thank you for helping me."

On the short ride to the tiny house, Robin once again became aware of how fatigued her body was. She tried to convince herself Marcus wasn't really in that much danger. She lit up with hope that he might already be at the house so she wouldn't have to go out to the woods and look for him. Just the thought of it made her even more exhausted.

They pulled up in front of the tiny house, narrowly missing one of the massive logs blocking their out-of-commission car. Penny finished their cigarette and peered across Robin at the house.

"Seems pretty dark."

"Peter had our power turned off. It's always dark."

"Dick move."

"One of many." She waved her hand at the massive logs in the street.

"Guess we should go check it out."

Penny pulled a beefy flashlight from their utility belt and turned it on. Robin followed them toward the house, any hope she had for Marcus actually being there rapidly dimming. They were so connected Robin swore if he was home she would've felt his presence.

When they reached the door, Penny stepped out of the way and said, "I'll let you unlock it."

"It's not locked," Robin said. "You'll see why."

Penny opened the door and stepped inside, shining the flashlight around the house's tiny interior. She paused, the pool of light capturing the tarp flapping in the breeze where the wall used to be.

"Your house is going to be filled with bugs," Penny said. "What are you going to do in the winter?"

Robin snorted. "Hopefully we won't be here. He removed the wall to 'expand the house.'" She made air quotes even though it was too dark for Penny to see her do it. "He said he was going to replace it but the cost of lumber was too high right now."

"I don't see him," Penny said. "Not too many places to hide."

"Nope. Can I see the light real quick so I can check upstairs?"

Penny handed Robin the flashlight and Robin scrambled up the absurd staircase, knowing he wouldn't be up there.

He wasn't.

The bed made her think of all the times she and Marcus had dozed off in a post-coital slumber. Would they ever be able to do that again? It seemed ridiculous to her that she even had to have that thought.

"No luck?" Penny said.

"Nope. To the woods we go, I guess."

"You can't think of anywhere else he might be?"

"His brother works at the brewery. I guess he might have gone there if he couldn't reach me by phone. But I think he still would've come by here to leave a note or something."

"It's only a couple minutes away," Penny said. "Wouldn't hurt to drive by and check it out. Those woods are going to be no joke at night."

"If you don't mind," Robin said. "That's where I was headed before I ended up at Mattie's."

They loaded back into the Bronco and headed to the brewery.

Pulling into the parking lot, Robin could already tell by the raucous atmosphere that something was off. Penny said they'd stay in the car.

Robin got out and walked toward the brewery. A drunk hippie with a lightning bolt shirt stood next to Jeremiah's goat, taunting it.

"Yeah, you're just a fucking smelly old goat. Probably just stand around here and eat trash people give you. You wanna smoke?" The hippie held a cigarette out to the goat but all he did was lick his lips and look at Robin. She wanted to say something to the guy but didn't have the energy. She went into the brewery.

It was packed. Everyone in attendance wore a lightning bolt shirt. Roger and Jeremiah were behind the bar. Roger looked forlorn. But Jeremiah seemed to be full of energy and was chatting with everyone with a smile.

Roger perked up a little when he saw Robin.

"Hey," he said. "Where's Marcus?"

"I was stopping in to see if you've seen him."

"I haven't. What happened?"

"I lost him in the woods." She quickly went about recounting her afternoon.

"Fuck. That's not good."

She motioned around her. "This isn't good either!"

"They just kept coming until everyone else was run out. We called the owners to see if we could kick them out but they said sales are sales. But they haven't, by the way, bought a damn thing all night. I think they just go out to the bike path and get high and hammered before coming back in."

"Well, look, I gotta go. I'm with a cop. They're going to help me find him. Long story. They're doing a favor for an old friend."

"Do you remember where you, uh, lost him?" Roger looked distraught.

Jeremiah moved a little closer as she told him about the dilapidated house and mud or quicksand or whatever it was.

"I think I know exactly where that is," he said. "If you went in near the Glen, then it probably seems like you went deep into the woods, but the way it winds, it's actually not too far behind this place."

"Too bad I can't borrow you," Robin said.

"It's not like I can't handle this myself," Roger said. "You won't be missing out on any tips."

Jeremiah nodded. "Can I bring Pan?"

Robin, unsure, said, "Most likely."

"Right on."

Jeremiah came out from behind the bar and followed Robin outside. The drunk hippie was nowhere to be seen. Jeremiah liberated the goat from its tether and they all walked to Penny's Bronco.

"This is Jeremiah," Robin said to Penny. "He knows an easier way to get where we need to go."

Penny crushed out their cigarette and said, "Lead the way."

They opened their door and scooted out, opening the rear door to an excited Conkles.

Robin, Penny, Jeremiah, Conkles, and Pan walked around the building because they didn't want to have to cut through all Peter's people in the brewery. There were more of them around back, filling the party patio, spilling onto the bike path and into the woods. Were these the people she'd heard yipping and braying in the reserve earlier? It made her more nervous. It seemed like they were celebrating something. She hoped that something didn't have anything to do with Marcus.

In the darkness beyond the security lights from the brewery, she could just make out a circle of them. They chanted something that sounded like "Jeremy! Jeremy!" She didn't think she wanted to know who Jeremy was.

They followed Jeremiah toward the woods, but Pan started freaking out with all the commotion. The goat leapt up into the air and looked like he wanted to butt something. Pan stood on his hind legs and came down with his chin tucked to his chest, ready to ram something, which caused Jeremiah to lose control of the leash. Pan ran toward one of the guys wearing a lightning bolt shirt. It was the drunk hippie who had been taunting Pan when Robin came into the brewery. The goat lowered his head and drilled the guy in the back of the knees and he went down.

One of the other yellow shirts saw this and shouted, "Get the goat!" and a group of them ran after Pan as he darted into the woods, a panicked Jeremiah close behind.

Penny, looking lost, Conkles happy and oblivious at her feet, said, "Well, fuck," and pulled a cigarette out of her pack.

Robin felt like breaking down and crying. It seemed like all hope was lost. She supposed she and Penny could venture into the woods, but she didn't see how she would recognize anything coming from this direction, especially in the dark.

She looked up at the moon twinkling in the sky. She closed her eyes and took a deep breath, trying to drown out all the commotion around her so she could think.

After taking a couple deep breaths, she focused on the group of people chanting "Jeremy!"

But they weren't saying "Jeremy."

She took another deep breath and tried to focus on what they were saying when she exhaled.

No. Definitely not "Jeremy." It sounded like they were saying "Jar me."

Her feelings of fatigue and hopelessness were now complemented by a sinking feeling.

She got Penny's attention and they followed her over to the group of chanting people.

"Jar me! Jar me! Jar me!" It was now obvious to her what they were saying.

She stood at the edge of the circle for a moment, observing.

Marcus was there in the middle, standing in front of a pyramid of jars. He looked crazed and ecstatic. Pieces of the very familiar robin's egg blue walls had been either glued or nailed to his chest, back, and upper arms so he still enjoyed a full range of movement. He would hand someone a jar and they would breathe into it before he quickly screwed the lid on and presented it back to them.

"That him?" Penny asked.

"'Fraid so."

"Need my help?"

"Maybe if you could just give us a ride home? I'm so fucking tired. I don't think I can walk all the way there."

"Sure thing."

Robin parted the crowd. Marcus didn't notice her until she grabbed his arm.

"Hey!" he said. "Glad you finally decided to show up!"

"What happened to you?" She grabbed a piece of the house attached to his arm and pulled on it, his skin pulled with it and she let go. "Come on, Marcus. We need to get home."

"No way. I got a lot more jars to do. These guys are so nice! They're all letting me jar them!"

"We need to go … now."

"Back to the house?"

"Yes."

"Fuck. I love that place. We're never going anywhere, are we?"

She began pulling him back toward Penny and the brewery. The small crowd began booing Robin.

Robin mumbled, "Eat my ass," so none of Peter's sycophants could hear her.

"Can my friends come back with me?" Marcus said, sweeping the group with his eyes.

"Absolutely not," she said.

Startling sounds erupted as they walked away and she realized they were throwing the empty jars at them. Penny did nothing to stop them. They didn't seem aware that anything was even happening, or they didn't care.

Their group entered through the back of the brewery and walked through it. Penny picked up Conkles to carry the dog through the crowd and kept saying, "K-9 Unit," to try and keep the drunk or high people from petting Conkles. Marcus seemed like he didn't even realize Roger was working. Robin told Roger they'd found Marcus and were going home. The people were so thick that Robin knew when Roger craned his neck to look at Marcus he couldn't really see him, and for the better for the state Marcus was in.

Roger asked, "Is he all right? Should I stop by later?"

"If by all right you mean alive, yes, he's all right," Robin said. "We'd love for you to come over but we're exhausted." She felt guilty speaking for Marcus but all she wanted to do was sleep. She got the overwhelming feeling that Marcus was not tired. "Feel free to stop by tomorrow."

Penny and Robin shoved their way through the crowd. Robin dragged Marcus by the hand toward the door. The group made their way to Penny's vehicle and piled in without a word to each other.

A few moments later, Penny was pulling up in front of the house again, avoiding the log obstacle course. Eyes still wide, Marcus looked at the shack and said, "Home sweet home."

21

MARCUS WAS SO HURRIED TO exit Penny's vehicle he caught the edge of the Robin's egg blue wall stuck to his arm on the doorframe. There was a sickening ripping sound, but if it hurt, Marcus didn't seem fazed. He ran up the short sidewalk, threw the front door of the house open, and darted into its darkened interior.

"He seems happy to be home," Penny said.

Robin sighed. She felt defeated and terrified, but also too tired to care. Penny certainly didn't seem to care. Robin's mind raced with questions. What part of the house was Peter going to affix to her? Would Marcus return from whatever delusion he was living? Would they ever leave this town? And would they leave alive?

"Yeah," Robin replied. "Guess so." She exited the vehicle through the door Marcus had left open.

Penny said, "If you need my help, just go back to Mattie's place."

Robin wanted to tell them she needed help now but was too exhausted and didn't think Penny would help her if she was on fire. Instead, she only nodded at Penny and shut the vehicle's squeaky door. Penny did a twenty-point turn around to avoid the logs and pulled away, leaving Robin standing on the darkened street.

There were only a couple of street lights on their street but the overgrown tree in the front yard stopped any light from reaching the front yard or the house. Everything was quiet except for the trill of insects around her and the crinkling of the tarp covering the side of the house as a light breeze stirred it. Robin stood on the road in front of the house, staring at the darkened structure in a daze, unable to think of what to do next.

A tapping sound caught her attention. The noise was getting louder and closer. She realized the sound was coming from behind her and had stopped abruptly. The hair on the back of her neck raised as she slowly turned around.

A buck with massive antlers stood motionless in the road, staring at her. It was so still it reminded her of the cement statues people placed in their yard, but a lot bigger. It was less than fifteen feet from her. Every muscle in her body cemented into place and her heart hammered. Her fight or flight instincts fought one another and froze her in place. She was afraid to move. She didn't know if a buck would attack her or run off if she moved and she was terrified to find out.

After what felt like an eternity, the animal licked its nose, huffed, and continued down the road. She relaxed once the buck was far enough away that she knew she could make it to the house in time if it changed its mind.

As much as she hated the thought of going back into the house, she didn't have much option other than to sleep in the car. Besides, Marcus was in there. No matter what happened, she wouldn't abandon him. She hoped she could deprogram him but didn't know exactly what that entailed.

She walked up the sidewalk and into the house, pulling the door shut, but not bothering to lock it. The wall was missing. If someone wanted in there weren't really any obstacles.

The complete darkness was unnerving. She could hear Marcus. It sounded like he was in the loft.

"Marcus?"

"I'm in bed. It's great! I love this place."

Robin sighed. She reached out, sweeping her arms back and forth, trying to find the railing for the stairs.

Once at the top of the stairs she crawled into bed, knocking her wrist against something hard. She felt the object and knew it was one of the wall pieces from the house attached to Marcus. She lay down beside him.

Robin pulled gently on the wall piece. "Are you going to take these off?"

"Why? I like the house. Besides, I'm not sure if I can."

"It's not normal to have pieces of a house attached to your body."

"It should be. If people love their houses, they should keep a part of it with them all the time."

"What happened?"

"What do you mean?"

"When you made it to Peter's house."

"I don't know what you're talking about."

"When we went to the woods. We went off the normal path and found a house in the woods. You got stuck in some mud or something and you told me to run."

There was a beat of silence. "I don't know what you're talking about."

Her eyes had adjusted enough to the darkness that she could faintly see him. He was lying on his back, staring at the ceiling, smiling. His expression disturbed her.

"Look at me," Robin said.

Marcus turned his head toward her, his expression staying the same.

"What did Peter do to you?"

"Nothing. You're being silly. Just enjoy the house."

She grabbed a piece of wall attached to his forearm and gently pulled it, turning his arm so she could inspect it. It appeared to be glued to his skin with a yellow adhesive. She pressed on the adhesive and it was hard.

"Do you want some to glue to your arm?" Marcus asked.

"No."

"Don't you love the house?"

"I'm tired," she said. "I think we should get some sleep."

"Good idea. I need to get some more jars tomorrow. I'm all out."

Robin was too tired to remind him that, as long as they lived here, both of their businesses were done. She was asleep in seconds.

~

A knock and shuffling sound pulled her from a dreamless sleep. Normally she didn't wake to anything. It was even hard for an alarm to pull her from sleep. But something in her brain must have stayed hypervigilant even in unconsciousness. More shuffling and rustling noises and then another knock. It sounded as if it were coming from downstairs.

Marcus snored lightly beside her. She thought about waking him but thought it might be best to let him sleep. She slowly and as quietly as she could crawled out of bed and to the stairs. She strained to listen for any more sounds. The tarp crinkled. She heard some more shuffling sounds, which sounded like they were coming from the middle of the downstairs floor. Some kind of insect landed on her and she brushed it away with a shiver.

Shit, she thought, *what if a raccoon got into the house? Or even worse, a skunk.* There was faint scratching. As much as she dreaded it, she knew she had to run out any creatures that let themselves in. She thought about the buck from earlier. She tried to think if there was anything she should use as a weapon or shield.

The cast-iron pan.

They'd put their extra kitchen items that didn't fit in the tiny kitchenette—things they didn't want to get rid of—in the small storage room in the loft. She knew it was in an open box just beyond the door. Without a sound, she opened the door, feeling for the box and retrieving the heavy pan. Her hand also grazed a flashlight she'd forgotten about and she grabbed that too. It was difficult to hold the pan with one hand but it would pack a punch if swung hard enough. And it was big enough to shield her face if a skunk decided to spray her.

She'd fallen asleep with her cell in her pocket. She retrieved it and thumbed it to check the time. The screen stayed black and she remembered that it was dead and dropped it on the carpeted floor of the loft. She turned on the flashlight, shining it down the steps toward the middle of the downstairs. Nothing was there. A few seconds later she heard another knock. She couldn't be sure, but it sounded like it was coming from under the floor. She assumed her light would run off any critters in the house or at least expose them. But the sounds continued.

She began the descent down the stairs, careful not to knock her head, and struggled not to drop the cast-iron pan. One of the steps groaned when she stepped on it and the noises stopped. She froze, listening. A minute must have passed, her arm shaking under the weight of the pan, before the sounds started back up. She was sure to put her weight down slowly as she proceeded, hoping to avoid any more sounds.

She shone the light around once she reached the bottom of the stairs and found nothing out of the ordinary. No skunks or raccoons or opossums. No massive bucks. A long scraping sound definitely came from under the house. She could feel it in the wood beneath her feet.

Robin set the pan on the kitchen table, giving her wrist a rest. She opened the front door and retrieved the pan. The insects were growing silent as the end of the night was near. Soon it would be the birds' turn.

She used the light to see where she was walking and made her way to the side of the house. The grass was cold and covered in dew. She peeked around the side of the house when she made it there. The stick holding the crawlspace door was lying in the side yard, along with the piece of wood it held in place. It didn't look like an animal had knocked it down. It was a few feet from its normal location and looked like someone had deliberately removed it and tossed it to the side.

A faint sound of rhythmic rubbing came from the opening ten feet from her. She proceeded toward the opening with the pan held high, ready to bring it down swiftly if she needed to.

Robin squatted onto her haunches and shone the light in the opening. Less than five feet from her, in the darkness of the crawlspace, Peter held a hacksaw and was sawing through a pipe under the house, water spilling onto the muddy ground. He snapped his head in the direction of the light. The light reflected off his glasses and made him look like an overgrown insect.

Robin froze. Part of her wanted to run. Run back into the house and lock all the doors.

But what good would that do when they were missing an entire wall?

Every logic that would inform a rational individual had been dismantled ever since moving into this fucking house. It struck her how quickly she and Marcus had been reduced to fearful shadows of their former selves. Peter had systematically taken away everything they thought made them who they were.

What were they supposed to do?

Conform?

Fall in line?

That's what Marcus seemed to have done. Robin would be damned if she ended up a Peter sycophant, whether she had pieces of the house attached to her body or not. The only reason she'd buy a yellow shirt would be to burn it in infamy.

Peter shifted, turning the tightly clutched hacksaw toward Robin.

Robin swallowed, her dry throat clicking.

She had never felt this level of exhaustion before. Not just physically. She was drained mentally and emotionally. It was like her body and mind couldn't even get it together enough to produce adrenaline. She felt drunk or stoned, but not the good kind.

She raised the cast-iron pan in front of her and made a sound somewhere between a grunt and a snarl.

She kept the light shining in Peter's eyes.

She was drawn into the reflection in his glasses. Suddenly, she saw herself perfectly. It was ridiculous. Why was she here? The absurdity of the image in the glasses continued to draw her in. It wasn't even possible for her to see herself that clearly.

You're seeing what he wants you to see.

And that was prey. A victim. A small woman up in the middle of the night, wielding a frying pan against … what? Something all-powerful? Something supernatural?

She imagined waking up tomorrow morning next to Marcus. They'd make a breakfast of rations obtained from the hardware store. Then they'd get to work constructing a wall for the house. They'd wander around in the woods until they found their people. Then they'd all help Peter clean and fix his house, tend his yard. Some of them would go on rent runs. It'd be fun. Passing on the torture they'd endured. Wasn't it time they had their chance? What they lacked in financial or material wealth would be redeemed in clout. The harder they worked for Peter, the more they could impress him. Then they could move to the woods and disappear from society completely.

She shook that thought away. Simply being this close to Peter was enough to make her gag. She was never going to do anything to help this guy.

There was a sound from upstairs and Peter went bonkers. Robin was too lost in her revery or hypnosis or whatever the fuck it was to know what was going on.

She continued to clutch the cast iron but Peter was charging toward her so fast the only thing she could manage was to move out of the way and swat at the back of his head with the pan which, were she to be perfectly honest, was entirely too heavy for her to use effectively even if she wasn't bone tired.

She watched as a glistening Peter ran charging into the coming dawn.

Why was he glistening?

22

MARCUS WOKE UP FEELING AMAZINGLY content but in a fair amount of physical distress. Before even opening his eyes, he moved his hand to the other side of the bed, expecting to find the warmth of Robin's hip, but all he felt was the cool, slight dampness of the cotton sheet.

He opened his eyes, first noting it was still dark outside.

Some things came back to him. Like, he was home. How did he get here?

The last thing he remembered clearly was going into the woods with Robin. He got stuck in some mud and told her to stay back ... or run. He couldn't remember which.

Then he remembered the sound.

It had started in his head. It was of such a pitch and volume it removed all other thoughts. Something like a more felt-than-heard bass sound had kept him rooted where he was. He wanted to run or scream or something but felt utterly paralyzed.

Even thinking about that sound now made him queasy.

Things were hazy after that.

He had seen so many recognizable people from town, all of them wearing the lightning bolt shirts and not much else. He felt like he was on an amazing drug he'd never experienced before. It felt like the drunkest, happiest he'd ever been, with no nausea or looming hangover. These people pulled him from the mud and took him to the house. Around the house, he could see other people—some in yellow lightning bolt shirts, some in little more than rags—emerge from holes in the ground. Collectively they went about dismantling the house in the woods that looked like it had been there forever.

Charlie from the hardware store was there.

"This is made from parts of all the rentals in town!" he shouted. Marcus couldn't remember anyone speaking in a normal voice. Everyone was shouting, which lent itself well to the overall anarchic, festive atmosphere. Marcus believed him because Charlie was loud and spoke with complete authority, but something in the back of his brain told him this was not right. Or, rather, this was not what they'd been told. He and Robin had been told that Peter had built his house and used the scraps to remodel the tiny house. But that already felt like years ago, so he was probably misremembering.

Charlie, sweating and smelling like a pile of chopped onions, said, "He's got bigger plans now! A gated community on the edge of town for the elites! Big things are happening, bro!" Charlie reached out and slugged his arm. For the first time since moving here, he felt like he belonged.

He'd followed them through the hot and sticky night. There'd been a large fire and a feast. What was it they were eating? Was it goat? It might have been goat. His appetite had seemed insatiable. And the villagers were so generous, encouraging him to eat until he was full. Maybe they had been at the brewery at some point? At least outside of it.

Hazily, he recalled people yelling for him to jar them and he'd had a seemingly endless supply of jars. It was like heaven. All he wanted to do was jar. Part of him wished he could be back there, in that moment, right now.

A pain snaked through his stomach and he instinctively placed a hand over it.

That's when he discovered the blue plywood affixed to him.

Another pain shot through his stomach. Maybe whatever he'd eaten hadn't been properly prepared or maybe he'd drank too much even though he couldn't recall drinking anything.

He needed to get to the bathroom.

Hopefully that wasn't where Robin was. He imagined she was sitting downstairs in the living room, probably thinking about her knees. She hadn't been sleeping so well lately. If she could only love the house as much as he did. Maybe he could convince her this was all part of Peter's crazy plan. They'd always seen themselves as something like outsiders anyway and this felt about as far removed from a mainstream society as was possible.

He bashed his head going down the stairs, but his first thought wasn't "Fuck." It was "Thanks." He wanted to thank the house for teaching him to be alive. That's what pain was. A reminder you're still alive. A reminder you can still feel things. If he didn't feel like he was on the verge of shitting his bowels out, he would place a hand on the old wood of the staircase and take a moment of blessed silence to enjoy the comfort of the house.

He took the few steps necessary to get to the bathroom, feeling his way around in the dark. A mosquito bit his cheek while another flew into his ear. What a miracle it was to be surrounded by so much nature. Forgetting they didn't have power, he tried to flick on the light, realized light was just a luxury when it didn't come on, thrust his shorts down, and practically dived onto the toilet, his bowels letting go immediately.

It felt like pure liquid and smelled rancid, as if he'd eaten seafood gone bad. He thought he heard some commotion going on under the house but figured it was just in his head. Or maybe some critter had come in through the crawlspace door. They really needed to do something about that. Or not. Nature implied abundance.

His bowels tightened and released again.

He hadn't had a shit this holy in a while. It felt like it was emptying him out, purifying him. As he endured the diminishing waves of pain and release, he thought about his and Robin's future in this house, in this town. Even though he could barely remember the events of that evening, he was certain he'd never felt more alive. That's why they'd moved here, wasn't it? To get outside and experience nature. To mingle with townies that were unlike most of the other townies in places dotting this part of the country.

He wiped, which was really just soaking up liquid shit, and flushed the toilet.

Something wasn't right.

THE LANDLORD

It seemed like it just emptied. He heard a splash somewhere under the bathroom floor.

Something else to fix, he supposed. He was pretty sure he and Robin had decided they weren't going to contact Peter about doing anything anymore, but now he couldn't remember why that was. Peter seemed like a great guy. Marcus really didn't want to bother him with something so trivial. He probably had way more important things to do. Peter was like the glue that held this town together. Land*lord?* More like land*friend.* He provided working-class people like him and Robin with affordable housing to strike a balance between the renters and the wealthy landowners around town. Peter volunteered his time and energy to make Little Falls a more equitable place.

He heard Robin scream, followed by a loud metal *clang.*

After taking a few steps to the front of the house, he saw her darkened silhouette outside the open front door, staring toward the huge tree in the front yard. It took him a moment to realize a pan lay on the brick sidewalk. The birds were chirping and the sky was a few shades lighter than night. Dawn was imminent.

When he got outside, he didn't ask what she was screaming about.

A skinned goat carcass hung from the tree, its blood dripping onto the dark soil below.

23

"WE HAVE TO MOVE," ROBIN said. "I don't care what it takes. We'll go see Roger tonight when the brewery opens. We can stay with him. Or we can stay with Mattie. I'm sure she wouldn't mind. She hates Peter too."

"I don't hate Peter," Marcus said.

Robin's exhaustion was never-ending. She and Marcus sat across from one another at the kitchen dinette. She turned and stared out the window and at the rooftops with their lightning rods. Then she focused on the exceptionally tall houses in the distance. She hadn't noticed until now that the houses being built in the new subdivision on the edge of town were several stories tall. Had that happened recently? She wasn't sure she'd noticed them from their place before. They loomed over all the houses in Little Falls. Almost as if they were stunted skyscrapers. Who would need a house that tall? What was even the point of making them so tall when it seemed like there was plenty of land available?

She shook her head and tried to clear her thoughts. They'd just finished burying the goat carcass in the backyard before any of the neighbors woke up. She was surprised her screams hadn't stirred them from sleep. Or maybe the neighbors knew what had happened and didn't want to get involved. Or ... they were already involved. All of it made her head spin. She didn't know who to trust anymore.

They'd found a rusty shovel in the shed and worked as quickly as they could. The shovel was garbage and they could've dug a grave quicker with their hands. The fact that they had to stop frequently to furiously scratch their multitudinous mosquito bites didn't make things go any easier. After digging two feet down they gave up and shoved the goat's remains into the hole and covered it with dirt. Robin was certain the hole wasn't deep enough and the carcass would begin to smell. That would attract other animals.

Now they were sweaty, covered in dirt and blood, and smelled like wild animals. The town was waking up around them and, thanks to the missing wall, they could hear it all: birds singing, cars driving by, the neighbor's dog that never stopped barking once the sun was up. She was certain the twitching nerve below her left eye was keeping time with the barking dog and she was starting to wonder if she was going to have a stroke.

Robin was too tired to argue with Marcus. She loved him but couldn't stay in this town another night. She didn't care what it took. She was leaving ... with or without him. Something was happening in Little Falls. More than Peter, more than Peter's sycophants, more than the neighbors acting like nothing was wrong, more than whatever happened to Marcus in the woods. Robin wasn't sure what it was, but for some odd reason, she couldn't stop thinking about the new subdivision being built on the edge of town. Something forgotten was nagging her but she couldn't put her finger on it. Like a forgotten dream.

"I can't stay here any longer," she said. "There's something wrong with this town and the people who live here and I'm not sure if it has something to do with Peter or if it's something bigger than Peter. And I know what I saw last night. I don't think he's human."

Marcus laughed. "Come on, Robin. Listen to yourself. You sound paranoid. Peter is just our landlord." He laughed again. "Are you trying to say there's some ... *ancient evil*—" he made air quotes with his fingers when he said ancient evil "— in this town trying to take over. Ridiculous."

Robin reached across the table and grabbed a piece of wall stuck to Marcus's arm and shook it. "This is ridiculous!" She let go. She shouted and spoke slowly, "You have pieces of a wall glued to your body and you don't seem to care!"

"I like the house." He stroked the wall piece she'd touched.

"What about the guy in the woods? You don't think you'll end up like him? Living in the woods with a mailbox nailed to your chest?"

"I'm sure he loved his house too."

"STOP GASLIGHTING ME!"

The couple sat silently, staring at one another. Minutes ticked by before Robin spoke.

"I'm going to see Roger when the brewery opens. Besides ... someone probably needs to tell Jeremiah to stop looking for his goat. If Roger can't help, then I'm going to Mattie's. It's up to you whether you want to come with me or not."

"Okay," he said. Marcus waited a beat before adding, "Why don't you get cleaned up and I'll make breakfast."

She nodded, slowly pushed away from the table, and made her way into the small room that housed their clothes. She gathered clean clothes while Marcus banged around in the kitchen.

Marcus retrieved a pan and rummaged around in the refrigerator. He was still pulling food from the darkened fridge when she passed him on her way to the bathroom.

Robin flipped the switch in the tiny bathroom. The light didn't come on.

"Of course," she said. "At least the stove is gas."

She set her clothes on the closed toilet lid and turned the shower handle all the way to hot. Water trickled out of the faucet. She sighed. Just one more reason to leave. She pulled the handle to switch the water to the shower head. It took forever but finally cold water trickled out from the shower head. She resigned to only washing her body. There was no way there was enough water pressure to wash any shampoo out of her hair. Instead, she wetted her hair, trying to at least rinse the sweat from her scalp. She hurriedly dried herself when she was finished, brushed through her tangled hair, and dressed. She dotted her mosquito bites with calamine lotion and asked Marcus if he wanted some for his, but he never answered.

He was eating some eggs and drinking coffee when she entered the kitchen, the hand not using a utensil scratching the large purple welts of the mosquito bites. Some of them were bleeding. A plate of eggs and a cup of coffee sat on her side of the table. She was about to ask how he managed to make coffee without power but spotted the kettle on the stove. She fell upon the food like a ravenous animal, even though she wasn't sure the eggs were safe to eat since they hadn't been refrigerated for some time. She hadn't realized how hungry she was until the first bite of food hit her stomach and she was finished eating before Marcus.

Marcus didn't look at her while she ate. He was already feeling guilty but he didn't have a choice. He couldn't leave Little Falls. *They* couldn't leave Little Falls. Marcus didn't know how to tell her they weren't leaving. Peter told him this would happen, and he'd told him what to do when it did. Although he couldn't remember if Peter told him this in person or not. Sometimes it was like Peter spoke directly to his brain. Peter was such a great guy that he'd even given him the tools he'd need. He really did think of everything. Marcus took slower and slower bites of his eggs. They didn't taste too strange to him. Maybe a little bitter. He was glad Robin had scarfed hers down.

Robin was starting to feel even more tired, which she didn't think was possible. Her head felt heavy and her eyelids kept falling as she watched Marcus eat. The exhaustion was finally catching up to her, she told herself. She noticed Marcus had stopped eating. He was staring at his plate, the fork sliding from his limp hand, drool falling from his lower lip. The state he was in struck her as odd, then she had a moment of panic before she slumped forward face-first onto her plate.

Marcus was glad she hadn't fallen on the floor as he slowly slid from his chair, hitting his head on the table on the way down. The strike to his skull hurt, but that was the last thought he had before the world went black.

24

APPROACHING THE LARGE, SECLUDED HOUSE, Marcus had the vague sense that it was his. His and Robin's. Mature trees surrounded the property, casting the yard in cool shade. He didn't know what fortuitous event brought him here and didn't want to think about it. It felt too good to be true. Things were finally working out. He felt good. It felt like meeting Robin for the first time. He had found something and didn't want to let it go. He walked into the house, surprised to find all the lights off.

"Robin!" he called. "You here?" This house was so large she wouldn't have necessarily heard him pull up or open the door. She was probably locked away in her art nook.

His phone vibrated with a text: "It's late. I'm in bed."

Marcus looked through the house, toward the large French doors that opened onto the patio and pool deck. The window was black and now he realized how dark the house had been. He flipped on a light. He guessed it was probably time for him to go to bed too. A wave of fatigue washed over him.

He began walking toward the bedroom, but each time he entered another room, it wasn't the room he thought it was. He supposed they'd had the house designed this way but was having trouble finding the logic of it in the present moment. Every room he went into was lit in a liminal way, not bright and very empty, making them all look slightly alien or out of time. Always budget-conscious, he thought about turning off all the lights but rationalized they were probably LED things that didn't take much energy. Still, whatever "mood" they were trying to create was off-putting and depressing. He walked through piss-yellow bathrooms, down innumerable hallways lit a sick brown-green, up and down several flights of stairs, bathrooms with multiple doors, kitchens with no appliances, bedroom after bedroom. He wanted to run, but the more he tried, the more leaden he felt.

Panic set in. He was starting to think he'd never find Robin. All he wanted to do was strip off his clothes and climb into the soft, warm bed with her.

"Robin!" He wasn't a loud person, but he yelled this. Or at least he tried. It felt like his voice was locked in his throat. The terror became more real and he fought to shout anything, make any kind of noise whatsoever.

"Robin!"

He kept trying to verbalize anything but his voice sounded like a deaf-mute person's.

"Robin!"

He opened another door, still trying to find Robin. It opened onto blackness. After taking a step, he realized he'd made a horrible mistake and now felt like he was falling down the stairs.

"Marcus!"

Once the initial disorientation passed, he realized it was Robin shaking him and calling his name.

He'd been dreaming.

He raised himself up on his elbow and turned to face her. He was lying on the kitchen floor. The pieces of the house affixed to him still made movement a little awkward, but he was getting used to it. In the end, he supposed, it would probably be beneficial.

"I just had the strangest dream," he said.

Robin didn't respond. She seemed shaken. He took a look around and noticed something else had changed.

"Have … have all the walls been taken?" he said.

"It must have happened while we were out!" she yelled. "When I came to, AFTER YOU DRUGGED ME, I'm pretty sure there were people surrounding the house."

"What were they doing?"

"I don't know, watching us sleep, I guess. Whatever they had planned WHILE I WAS ROOFIED!"

"That's crazy."

"That you drugged me, or that there were people surrounding the house?" She waved her hand dismissively at him. Robin chuffed out a sarcastic sound and said, "After everything that's happened, you think *that's* crazy."

He reached out a hand and placed it on her forearm but she quickly shook it off.

"I wouldn't describe what's been happening as *crazy*," he said. "A bit unconventional maybe."

"What the fuck happened to you in those woods?"

"I don't know what you mean."

"Before I left you behind in the woods, you were on the same page as me. We were both trying to get the hell away from here, find out what's wrong. Now you're like one of *them*."

Now it was his turn to chuff out a sarcastic laugh. "What do you mean by *them*. The people in town?"

"No, not everyone in town. You know who I'm talking about. The lightning rod people. The Peter people."

He smirked and said, "Oh, you mean the *Renters*." He capitalized this last word in his head. It made them sound like they had a common purpose. A plight. Or like a band or gang or something. "Tell me again how we're not like them."

Now she seemed to be getting even more upset at him. "These are not ordinary renters. They're Peter's people. You know that as much as I do. Do you want *us* to become Peter's … I don't even know what they are. Followers? Disciples? Slaves?"

From outside, that bizarre whistle clearly rang through the quiet. Robin flopped back on the floor and said, "Jesus, not now. What the fuck time is it? I don't know what time it is. My phone hasn't been working and we don't have power anymore."

"That's what I wanted to say. I didn't roofie you. Why would I roofie both of us? I think the eggs were off because of the lack of refrigeration." Marcus said this lying on his back staring at the ceiling.

He glanced at Robin just to make sure she was really there. He was still having trouble shaking that dream. That's when he noticed what looked like roofing shingles covering both her knees. She hadn't mentioned anything about it. He wasn't going to bring it up right now. She would most likely think he had roofed her specifically so he could attach the shingles to her knees. He knew Peter was in the vicinity and didn't want to do anything to set her off.

"Morning, folks!" Peter called from the street. "You seen the little guy around?"

"Fuck off, asshole!" Robin yelled.

"You're not a nice person," Peter said. "I wanted to let y'all know that rent's due."

Robin stood up. "How are we supposed to pay rent when you've taken every way we have to make money, including my knees!"

Oh, so she must have noticed, Marcus thought, surprised she hadn't said anything about it.

"You know what, I don't know what kind of psychopath comes around this early in the morning to tell us the rent is due, but we might just not pay it this month. Or the next month. Or ever again. What are you going to do, evict us?"

His happy demeanor slipped. "You really, really don't want that to happen," Peter said.

"Why? Because it would be worse than this? We're practically living outside. People living in tents are better off than us."

"And, honey, I don't know when three in the afternoon was ever considered early. I have to go find my cat," Peter said. "You'll see how much better this is in the end. You have to trust the process."

"Fuck off," Robin practically snarled.

"Such a nasty person," Peter muttered.

25

BOTH OF THEM WERE RATTLED about Peter's threat. Robin was disturbed by the fact they'd slept half the day away. She wanted to be angry with Marcus for drugging them both—even though he claimed otherwise—but it seemed the least of her worries at the moment.

All the food in the refrigerator had gone bad and they decided to leave the fridge closed instead of cleaning it out. It was all they could do at the moment to stick it to Peter. Marcus ground some coffee beans in a mortar and pestle, loaded up the Moka pot, and heated it up on the gas stove. For some reason, it tasted especially good. Maybe because it felt like one of the last remnants from a simpler time.

They were finally able to assess what had been done to the house while they were asleep on the kitchen floor. The roof was still there, but the shingles had been removed. A couple of them had, apparently, been affixed to Robin's knees. All the walls had been removed. They scratched various bug bites as they sat in lawn chairs on the back porch, sipping their coffee.

Even though she felt good and oddly tranquil, Robin knew she had to say something.

She looked at Marcus as he sipped his coffee and looked up at the sun peeking through the leafy canopy of their backyard. Birdsong filled the air. The fact that she loved their surroundings made this whole situation even worse. It made it seem cruel. Like the whole world was a massive rug-pull. Was it only okay to want things as long as what you wanted was exactly what most other people wanted? Was it really impossible to obtain any type of personal happiness without loads of money or making yourself or others miserable? This was the terrifying thought she couldn't get out of her head. And suppose they did suck this up, what would the outcome be? If they just gave up and began blindly following Peter like so many others in the town, would they get their walls back? Would he leave them alone? She didn't think so. She was pretty sure Peter's whole goal was to destabilize them and throw them off balance so they were too rattled to fight back. She was pretty sure she'd never hated anyone more passionately than she currently hated Peter.

Sadly, that was probably the only thing keeping her from turning her hate on Marcus. Sitting there and sipping his coffee and listening to birdsong like nothing was wrong made him seem like the most naïve simpleton in the world. And, yes, she finally admitted to herself, she hated him a little for that.

"So," Robin said, "no water. No electricity. No walls. No phone service."

Marcus sipped his coffee and said, "Kind of nice, isn't it?"

Robin nearly did a spit take with her coffee. "Fuck no! Are you kidding?"

"I don't know what we're supposed to do, so I guess I'm just trying to … accept it."

"This is untenable. Please tell me you're not so brainwashed you can't understand that."

"Well, then I guess we can go back to jobs we hate, live in some dump in the city where we're breathing black mold and other people's germs, or the suburbs where we spend all of our time fixing up the house and yard for no one to notice ever. But, hey, at least we'll have a working toilet … maybe … most of the time."

It took her a couple of seconds to process a response to this.

"Everything isn't so black and white, Marcus. It's a landlord's duty to provide for basic human needs, at the very least."

"Do we really *need* more than this?"

"Yes! *I* do. *You* do too, you just don't realize it. Also, does providing for basic human needs include threats and intimidation? Do you want to wake up to a skinned sacrifice outside the door every morning? Is that a basic human need?"

Marcus waved it away. "Ah, somebody was just goofin'."

Robin was closer to losing her shit on Marcus than she had been since meeting him.

"Do you want to talk about what happened this morning?" she said.

"What do you mean?"

"Well, we were both sitting at the breakfast table and just ... lost consciousness. You haven't even mentioned the fact that I have *fucking shingles* stuck to my knees. That's how I make my money. That's what I use to live. Speaking of which, I'm sure you've failed to notice, but there's not a single jar in the house."

"There are plenty of jars."

"But they're all used. You expressly told me that you don't reuse jars. So how are you going to sell the ones you have?"

"I'm pretty sure I can find a market in town."

Robin stood up and tossed her remaining coffee out into the overgrown lawn.

"All right, then. Get up. Gather your jars. We're going into town so you can sell them. Rent's due, remember? And we're technically violating the lease by doing it, but hey, laws and contracts don't mean shit anymore anyway. So get up. Chop-chop."

"Yeah, yeah. Let me finish my coffee."

Robin tossed her cup out into the yard and stalked into the house where she used the restroom in a toilet that emptied directly onto the ground below the house. She cleaned her face and took a whore's bath with wet wipes, which she also chucked down the waterless toilet. The lease said not to use them because they clog the plumbing, but the last time she checked, they didn't have any plumbing. When she was finished with that, she walked ten steps to retrieve the mail from the box that now lay on the ground, hoping irrationally for some kind of check in there. They still hadn't received their deposit from the apartment, so the idea wasn't really that far-fetched.

The only thing the box contained was a letter from Peter telling them their grass was too tall.

26

THEY GATHERED UP MARCUS'S "FILLED" jars, put them
in boxes, put the boxes in a lawn cart, and went into town. They
bought subpar sandwiches they couldn't afford from the grocery
store. Marcus had a sign on his cart that read "Artisanal Jarred Air."
So far, no one had even asked them about it. Robin had no idea what
she was trying to prove by making him do this. Maybe she was just
trying to exhaust him.

"Haven't sold a single jar yet," she said.

"People probably aren't home from work. They're busy with errands and stuff."

"We passed a whole group of retired people playing hackysack.
You could have hit them up."

"Ah, everyone knows retired people are poor."

"Even here?"

"Sure. Their budgets. Old people always have budgets. It's like
they know exactly how much money they need to live before they die.
Fixed incomes."

Robin stopped and turned her gaze on the tall houses in the distance. "Maybe we should try there," she said.

"Where? You're just, like, looking at the sky."

"The really big houses out on the edge of town. You can't see them?"

"I see the houses in town and, like, trees."

"Okay. Well, we're going there and you're going to try to sell your jars to the people who live there. Trust me, they have plenty of money."

"Sure. Sounds like they'd be into jarred essence. I want to stop at the hardware store first. I need some more empties. I was pretty sure I saw some there."

Robin had zero recollection of seeing any empty jars in the hardware store.

"Plus, I'd like to say hi to Charlie. He's really friendly."

Robin rolled her eyes and said, "Fine." Christ, she'd be exhausted before Marcus if the day continued like this.

The hardware store was only a block away and Robin stayed slightly behind Marcus pulling his sad cart of shit that nobody in their right mind wanted. How could she not have realized how completely delusional he was?

Marcus pulled the cart into the store, Robin following him. Charlie sat behind the counter reading a book called *Meat Photo* while a gray cat lounged on the counter in front of him.

He smiled that crazy smile when he saw them.

"Hey! Robin and Marcus! Long time, no see!"

"Hey, Charlie," Marcus said.

Charlie rushed around from behind the counter and pulled both of them into a hug. He didn't smell great.

"What can I do you for?" Charlie said.

"I'm looking for more jars. Our landlord did some renovating and I guess he must have got a little carried away."

Charlie made a face that said he knew exactly what Marcus was talking about and said, "Well, you know, Peter's a very busy man. Even with all the help he's been getting, I think he's still a little overwhelmed, if you ask me."

"For sure," Marcus said.

Robin stood there, stewing, hating them both.

"As it so happens," Charlie said. "These just came in yesterday." He motioned to the wall behind the counter that clearly contained the exact amount of jars Marcus was most likely missing.

"Oh, those are *perfect*," Marcus said. "That's the same exact kind I use. They seem to be a hit, even though it's really the essence that people buy them for."

"These are a new item, so unfortunately I can't sell them any cheaper than thirty bucks a jar."

Robin strangled a guffaw. And was gobsmacked when Marcus reached for his wallet.

"I only have money for maybe three or so," he mumbled.

Robin grabbed his hand. "Come on," she said. "We need to go."

"But—" Marcus began.

"Trust me," she said. "They'll still be here later."

"I wouldn't be so sure about that," Charlie said. "Marcus's jars were a big hit the other night. I'm sure we already have one other copycat in town."

He glanced toward the register and Robin noticed a jar with the word "Basemeant" written on it.

"It's you, right?" Robin said. "You're the copycat?"

Charlie just waggled his eyebrows and said, "Well, seeing as I get such a robust wholesale discount on jars, I couldn't pass up the opportunity. You were here for the comedy show the other night. You know I'm trying to diversify. And I think I'm doing a pretty good job at it."

"Marcus, we're leaving," she said.

Marcus looked at Charlie and shrugged his shoulders in an infuriating "What else can I do" gesture.

They walked for what felt like miles even though she was pretty sure the entirety of the town was under two miles. The houses in the distance grew larger and taller. Part of Robin was genuinely curious to go door-to-door in this neighborhood. She wanted to know who lived here.

As they turned onto the street leading into the neighborhood, Robin's heart sank.

A tall black wrought iron fence extended in either direction for as far as she could see.

She took a deep breath and said, "Don't fuck with me, I just want to know one thing."

Marcus nodded and said, "Okay. What is it?"

"Do you see the houses back there?"

"Of course," he said.

"Would you say they're normal houses?"

"Nah. Too tall."

"Thank you."

They continued walking toward the gate. A bronze plaque announced it as "Founders' Colony. Established 1666." They heard construction sounds coming from a plot of land relatively near the gate. The house going up looked a lot like their tiny house, the same color blue, only it was really tall. Like taking the raw materials from their house through this gate somehow made them more abundant and bountiful.

She ran her hand over the plaque and mumbled, "Who do you think they're trying to keep out?"

27

ROBIN STAYED FAR BEHIND MARCUS, hoping no one knew they were together. Who was she kidding? One look at the state of both of them, covered in random pieces of the tiny house, and it was obvious they were a pair.

Marcus pulled the yard cart, headed in the direction of home, the jars clinking against one another as the cart rolled over the broken concrete of the sidewalk. He stopped at every house and knocked on the door. If anyone answered he'd gleefully try to sell them one of the remaining jars. He hadn't been able to sell even one.

Robin lulled behind, pretending to be engaged with the flowers and overgrown foliage a couple of doors back. She observed the townspeople who answered their doors. Most of them acted as if Marcus was a Girl Scout peddling cookies, although they never bought anything from him, and others, rightfully so, seemed to be disturbed by Marcus's appearance, staring at the pieces of walls affixed to his body, although none of them mentioned it. She noted the oblivious residents' homes were adorned with a lightning rod, and many of them wore the yellow shirts with lightning bolts on them.

When Marcus reached the intersection of their street he called to Robin, "I don't think I'm gonna get a sale today!"

Robin hurried toward him so they didn't need to shout to one another. "That's okay," she said when she caught up to him. "Let's head home. I'm gonna need your help with something."

They walked home together down the center of their street. The first thing they noticed when they were within view of the tiny house was that all of the windows had been removed. All that was left of their house were the studs and the floors. Everything they owned was on full display.

"Hey," Marcus said, "it looks like Peter finally installed that central air he was talking about."

Robin wanted to ask him what central air he meant. Peter had definitely not mentioned anything about central air. She didn't know what to say, so she didn't bother. She was pretty sure if she said anything she'd either start crying or screaming and she wasn't sure she'd be able to stop if she started.

Robin walked through the front yard and headed to the side of the house. Marcus dropped the yard cart handle once it was in the yard and followed her. She marched through the overgrown grass and straight toward the shed in the backyard.

Marcus spotted the open hole in the backyard where they'd buried the goat. "Looks like Jeremiah came and got Pan. He's such a good goat dad. I bet he gave him a proper funeral."

Robin shoved a plastic trashcan littered with holes out of the way. She picked up a metal fence post and threw it into the yard, along with pieces of warped scrap wood and a moldy bag of mulch in a sun-bleached bag. Marcus watched her as she grabbed something hidden in the long grass, gave it a yank, and a metal ladder emerged.

She tossed the ladder back down on the ground, clear of the overgrown patch of grass. "There," she panted.

"What do we need that for?" Marcus asked.

"I have a feeling the answers to our problems are in that new housing addition. And if I can't get out of Little Falls, then we're getting inside Founders' Colony one way or another."

28

MARCUS AND ROBIN SAT AT the dinette table, eating crackers and chips. The food was the only thing they had left that didn't require cooking or refrigeration. The sun was setting and neither of them had spoken much in the past couple of hours, both reflecting or contemplating or just being at peace with not thinking at all.

Robin could see tons of mosquitos flying around them. She was constantly smacking herself to kill the damned things and it was really starting to get on her nerves. She felt like ripping her skin off and handing it to the bugs. She thought she would feel better if she did. The air was stagnant and humid and she was covered in sweat and grime and now the bugs were making a feast of her and she was certain that every bite would get infected if she scratched them. She could see the bugs were eating Marcus alive too but he didn't seem to care. Periodically, he would scratch a bite, but he wasn't too bothered by the swarm. He just sat there eating his chips as if the house wasn't in shambles and he wasn't covered in random pieces of the house and bug bites and they hadn't been through the shit they'd been through in the last month. Robin hated to admit it, but his aloofness was irritating her. How could all of this not bother him? She wanted to grab him by the shoulders and shake him until he snapped out of it.

She smacked another mosquito and sighed.

Marcus stuffed the last handful of chips into his mouth, crumpled the bag, and let it drop on the floor. He wiped his greasy hand on his shirt and declared, "No more chips."

"We should get going," Robin said.

"Where are we going?"

Robin didn't bother answering him. "Help me with the ladder."

"Okay."

Robin walked through a gap in the studs and Marcus followed. A piece of the house nailed to his arm got hung up on a stud and he yanked his arm free. There was still enough daylight to see the ladder lying in the yard.

Robin grabbed one end of the ladder. "Grab the other end. I'll lead."

Marcus did what she told him.

They left the yard, maneuvered around Peter's logs in the road, and headed toward Founders' Colony. By the time they'd arrived at the gates it was full dark.

29

PART OF ROBIN ALMOST FELT bad for making Marcus go through with this. He hadn't said much on the walk through town and through the small, well-manicured nature preserve left over from the area they'd undoubtedly developed for this neighborhood so the residents could still get the "woodsy vibe" of the town. Marcus's eyes were open wide as he stared at the bright lights beyond the gates. Lights weren't the only things capturing their senses. There was raucous laughter and pulsing music. The people who lived on the other side of the fence clearly knew how to have a party.

"Remember," Robin said, "the best things happen when you don't have a plan."

"I just hope they accept us. Maybe one of them will let us rent a room or something."

Robin could only stare at him in open-mouthed dismay. He still wasn't getting it. She bit her tongue. She didn't know what she had planned after they gained admittance, but it certainly wasn't to try and make friends with these people. In her mind, sending them a message was going straight to the source of the problem. She felt like Peter was probably more of a symptom.

Marcus pointed at the really tall house closest to them. The one they'd seen earlier.

"Maybe that one's being built for us. Maybe that's what Peter's been doing with the walls and stuff from our house."

Robin could no longer hold her tongue. "I thought we had gotten to know each other pretty well, but how fucking naïve are you?"

"What do you mean?"

"Do you always think there's some pot of gold at the end of the rainbow? I thought that's why you'd gone into business on your own. I know it's why I did. I knew that no matter how hard I worked for whatever person or company, I was always going to be worth more and paid less than them. There is no secret reward system in place. If you're paying rent, people are going to get as much from you as they can while offering nothing they're not legally bound to give you. Peter is a shitty person taking advantage of people for who knows what reason."

"I just … I don't know … I really like it here."

"I do too. Except for these people. And Peter. They are the ones who make it bad."

Marcus sat down heavily in the grass and said, "I'm sure if we make it known to Peter that things have to change, he'll work with us."

"He won't. He's not a good person and he's somehow in cahoots with these people, who are even worse."

"I hate this," Marcus said before leaning back against the fence. He quickly shot away from the fence. "Fuck! I think it's electrified."

"Goddammit," Robin said.

"What now?"

"The ladder's made out of fucking aluminum."

"Oh."

Marcus sounded so dejected Robin momentarily considered saying fuck it and just going back to the house, or what was left of it, and just … what? Wait until their lease was up? They hadn't even been here two months, even though it felt like a lifetime. There was no way they could survive the winter. The house couldn't even act as a shelter. And it wouldn't be long before Peter took everything, including the shit-filled crawlspace.

They heard a rustling in the nearby undergrowth. Robin cursed herself for not bringing anything other than the ladder. Not that they'd ever been ones to keep anything approaching an arsenal. They could have at least brought some kitchen knives or something.

Peter emerged from the darkness, his eyes glowing with a sickly yellow light. He was naked except for some kind of rustic loincloth and appeared to be smeared in either blood or shit. It was impossible to tell with the lack of light. But the stench emanating from him indicated it was possibly both.

"You don't want to bother those people." Peter's voice was low. He continued creeping slowly toward them.

"Oh, hey, Peter." Marcus seemed unaware of the potential risk of their situation.

"Stay the fuck back," Robin said. "Who are those people?"

Peter dramatically gestured toward the sign. "I think it's obvious, isn't it? Those are the founders of Little Falls."

"That's impossible," she said.

"It's ... uncommon. Not impossible."

"Is that why you're doing this? Do you serve them?"

Peter's crazy smile came back, the light in his eyes dimming enough to make Robin wonder if she'd imagined it all to begin with.

"Everyone in this town serves them," Peter said. "I help them to ... show their devotion."

"You're absolutely insane, aren't you?"

This time he actually barked out a laugh. "I'm the sanest person you'll ever meet. When in the presence of gods, I dropped to my knees and have done everything I could to stay in their light and good graces. Wouldn't you like to stay here for eternity? Why take a gamble on the mainstream gods? Why wonder about an afterlife if you can have life eternal? We don't want heaven. We want paradise on earth."

"But only behind that fence, right? Aren't those the only people it's for?"

"Do you trust commoners to make their own decisions? Doesn't it stand to reason that the people who founded the town know what's best for it? Besides, they go beyond the fence every day. They walk among you to remember societal pleasures. But behind these gates ... we're something altogether different. The Founders' Colony is our soul, something to be kept pristine and untouched."

"You could just let us leave and we won't have to do anything to them."

"Marcus?" Peter said. "Do you want to leave?"

"Nah. I'm good here."

Robin's face burned with rage. How was he not aware of what was happening? How was he not aware of how bad this situation was? She was beginning to think she'd moved in with a real dud.

"I'm so glad you had a change of heart," Peter said. He turned his attention back to Robin. "Maybe you could have a change of heart too. Realize all the infinite possibilities that await you."

"The only thing I want is to be free and for you to go to jail for a very long time."

Peter threw his head back and laughed exactly like the villain he had increasingly proven himself to be. "Look to the sky. You'll learn that my rods will never let anything happen to me."

Robin scanned the perimeter of the horizon. The tips of many lightning rods were glowing. She tried to look away as fast as possible but not before it felt like something was squeezing her head from the inside. She'd never felt anything like it. She wondered if this was what a stroke felt like.

She heard Peter bark, "Fuck!" Like that, the stranglehold was gone from her brain.

Peter had backed away.

He threw his hands up in front of him but not quick enough to avoid whatever was being hurled at him. It glanced off his forehead and Robin was still close enough to him to see what it was in the dim light coming from within the fence.

A beer bottle.

She turned to see Roger and Jeremiah, side by side, each of them reaching into bags strapped bandolier-style over their shoulders. Jeremiah seemed to be wearing some sort of animal pelt and Roger looked like he was in a nearly blacked out state. They advanced toward Peter like machines, drilling bottle after bottle at him until, unable to take the onslaught, he turned and ran back into the darkness.

Robin allowed herself one quick glance toward the lightning rods and noted they had all gone dark. Thankfully, she hadn't gone full Marcus.

"Oh, hey, guys," Marcus said. "What's up?"

"Something's very wrong with Marcus," Robin said.

30

THE GROUP HAD TAKEN THE ladder and retreated from the
housing addition. They walked a couple blocks to a small park so
Robin could rehash what had taken place. Being so close to where
Peter was made her a little nervous to talk. She got the feeling they
were being watched and listened to when they were close to the fence.
She was sure there were cameras near the entrance. Besides, there was
a street light on the road outside the park and they all could see each
other better.

"I think you're right," Roger said. He shifted his weight from one
foot to the other and nearly fell, still intoxicated. "I think we need to
get in there and fix whatever they did to Marcus and find the person
who slashed *my* tires."

"Oh no, not your car too." She sighed. "The fence is electrified,"
Robin reiterated. "I don't think there's any way to get in there." She
approached Roger and retrieved a beer bottle from his bag, cracked
it open, and took a large swallow.

"That's what I'm talking about," Jeremiah said and pulled a beer

132

from his bag. He twisted the bottle cap off and drank the whole bottle in one go.

Marcus stared off in the direction of the addition and said dreamily, "I bet if we ask Peter he would let us in."

Robin rolled her eyes, shook her head, and took another drink.

Jeremiah rubbed his chin and stared at the ground. "I think ... I might know a way in."

He had everyone's attention.

"It might be nothing," he said, "but at the back of the development, when they first started building the houses, there was a large black ... building, I guess. I'm not sure. It wasn't as large as the houses. And it didn't have any windows or doors. The walls were all shiny and we thought it was made of solar panels, but we were pretty drunk. When you got close to it you could hear a low humming sound."

"You got close to it?" Robin asked.

"Yeah," he said. "A few of us rode our bikes out there one night after work to dick around and drink when they were working on the first few houses. At the time I just assumed it was a generator or some sort of power source. I mean, they had to power their tools somehow, right?"

"Yeah," Roger said, "that makes sense."

"We should check it out," Robin said.

Jeremiah added, "It might be inside the fence now. I haven't been back there since. The cops found out we were back there somehow and came to the brewery and threatened to have us all arrested for trespassing. But it was all the way at the back, where the farmer's field touches the property. I can't imagine they wanted it anywhere they could see it."

"Let's go," Robin said. She gestured to Jeremiah to lead the way.

"It's gonna take a bit to get there. The easiest way is to walk all the way to the edge of town and take the last road out to the field behind the addition and double back."

Marcus said, "I don't think Peter will be happy if we leave town."

"What Peter doesn't know won't hurt him ... or us," Robin said. "Besides, it doesn't actually leave the town limits, right?" She let out a panicked laugh. "Because ... once you've signed the lease, you can't leave, right?"

Jeremiah silently nodded his head.

Marcus closed his eyes and breathed a deep sigh of relief. "Good."

"Marcus," Roger said, "fuck that d-bag. You're your own man. You don't have to answer to anyone."

Marcus gave Roger a spacey smile, like he wasn't really listening or didn't care.

Robin was growing impatient. "Let's go." She started walking toward the end of town, not looking back to see if any of the group were following her.

Jeremiah and Roger grabbed the ladder and the other three followed her.

~

When they reached the road at the edge of town they turned and headed north. Even out this far the group could see the lights and hear the music coming from Founders' Colony. They could also smell fire, and possibly some sort of cooked meat.

"It's a nice night for a barbecue," Marcus commented. "I'm really hungry. Maybe they'll let us have something to eat."

"Wow," Roger said, unenthusiastically. "He really is gone. Don't drink any Flavor Aid if they offer it."

"Yeah," Robin said.

No one else spoke until Jeremiah was certain they were in an area where they could walk through the cornfield and safely reach the black building. They all agreed not to speak until they reached their destination, in case someone were to hear them. Passing through the corn was plenty loud enough. Roger tripped over some mud clods a few times, but luckily the corn was dense enough that it broke his fall without him getting hurt. Something scratched Robin's leg. She wanted to curse at the stinging pain and could feel blood trickling down her leg but managed to keep quiet. At least the shingles protected her knees.

The group once again could hear music and people talking in the distance, the lights becoming visible again. Jeremiah signaled for everyone to stop, squatted down, and slowly crept forward.

Robin craned her neck to look through the stalks of corn. They'd reached the end of the cornfield and she could see the black building. It was a shadow, highlighted by a street light not too far from it. But it was inside the fence. The building did seem to be made of glass panels. There was also a paved road leading to it from a street within Founders' Colony, but it was separate from the houses.

"Now what do we do?" Robin whispered. "It's inside the fence."

Marcus pushed a leaf of a corn stalk to the side so he could see the building. He pointed at something. "Look," he whispered.

The rest of the group followed his finger to where he was pointing. They all spotted the colorful bundle of twisted wires flowing from the black building, down the road, and into the housing addition.

Roger said a tad loud, "It has to be powering the houses or something."

Jeremiah shushed him and whispered, "You've had too much to drink. You're talking loud."

"They're not going to hear us," Roger said. "They're having a party."

"What are we doing?" Marcus said.

"We can't get to it," Robin said. "It's inside the fence." She reached into Roger's bag and pulled out a bottle of beer, took a few steps to clear the corn, and launched the bottle over the fence and toward the black building.

The bottle sailed through the air but landed short and hit the ground hard enough to break with a "pop."

The other three joined her. They all grabbed the last of the beers and launched them at the building. Some landed short, but two hit their target and shattered the glass on the building.

Everything went dark and silent.

"Oh shit," Roger said. "Ha-ha!"

"Peter isn't going to be happy about this," Marcus said.

Jeremiah said, "Look, the lightning rods are glowing."

"No," Robin said. "Don't look at them. Nobody look at them." Robin waited for her eyes to adjust to the new darkness and avoided looking toward any lightning rods. She was thankful the sky was clear and the moon was full. A yellow shimmering light came from within Founders' Colony and Robin was sure it was a large bonfire.

"We don't have much time before they come back here," Jeremiah said.

"This is it then," Robin said. "Run!" She grabbed the ladder and ran for the fence.

31

THINGS HAPPENED FAST. ROBIN ASCENDED the rungs
of the ladder quickly, without getting electrocuted. Reaching the top
of the fence, she realized she hadn't planned on how to get down on
the other side. Still, standing at the top felt victorious. She took a
chance and let herself drop into some bushes surrounding the interior
of the fence.

"I'm goin' next!" Roger shouted and took a wobbly hold of the
ladder.

Whatever momentum they'd been feeling rapidly died as Roger
shakily ascended first one rung and struggled with the second one.
Then the night lit up as bright as noon.

And Roger was gone.

What the fuck? Robin thought.

She scanned the skyscape. One of the lightning rods closest to
them was glowing. She averted her eyes quickly, feeling the sticky tendrils of something inside her head in that brief glimpse.

Could that have possibly been what made Roger disappear? What happened to him? Where did he go?

"Roger!" Marcus called from outside the fence.

"I'll go next," Jeremiah said. He gestured toward the animal skin draped over his shoulders. "Magic goat hide."

Marcus watched nervously as Jeremiah quickly climbed the ladder. The night lit up again, but Jeremiah was still there a split-second later when the darkness returned. He climbed up onto the top of the fence and flipped off the sky with both hands. Maybe he was flipping off the lightning rods.

"Be careful, Marcus," Robin said through the fence.

Marcus turned toward her, smirked, knocked the ladder down and ran into the cornfield.

In a burst of unreasonable anger, Robin shouted, "I hope you drown in quicksand, motherfucker!"

She was met with Jeremiah's surprised reaction when she turned to face him.

"We should try and stay undercover," he said. "Keep to the shadows and keep quiet."

Glancing around the cloistered neighborhood, that seemed like both an easy and a difficult thing to do. Every yard was lush with shrubs and trees, the five and six-story houses rising from them. Each house was equipped with a lightning rod and, after Roger's disappearance, she now wondered what the true purpose of the lightning rods was. She imagined them like all-seeing eyes, cameras monitoring their every move. That would explain why Peter had always seemed to show up at the worst possible times. She also had to assume they contained some sort of laser. She had no idea if Roger had been relocated or vanquished altogether.

"Follow me," Jeremiah said, and she followed him into a small copse of trees.

"Do you think anyone saw us?" Robin asked.

"I don't think so." He motioned to a group of maybe twenty people who'd seemed to form some sort of search party in the street a couple blocks from them.

Robin noticed a few of the people in the group were wearing what looked like robes and it made them appear as though they weren't from town. Maybe they were from another country.

Elsewhere, the music returned and the regular kind of partying seemed to have returned in full force. The pulsing EDM and hysterics made a lot more sense after she got a good look at the people living here.

She was expecting elderly people. Surely it would take a lifetime to save up enough money to purchase one of these palaces. But everyone she saw seemed young enough to make her envious, and she wasn't exactly old. She wasn't a spring chicken at forty-four, but she definitely wasn't as young as the others appeared. The whole neighborhood felt like a frat party that was close to getting out of hand.

"What the fuck is this?" she muttered under her breath.

Jeremiah continued staring at the wandering throngs of young-looking people.

"Are their parents on vacation or something?" None of this made any sense to Robin.

"He's keeping them young," Jeremiah said.

"Who? Peter?"

Jeremiah leaned back on his heels and stroked his pelt with both hands.

"I don't know how," he said. "But he's doing something to keep these people young. I haven't seen a lot of these people in years. Thought they'd just kind of disappeared or moved away. I always thought people would be crazy to move away from here. I mean, like, unless you're able to move to a real place."

"That's impossible," Robin said, even though she was now starting to think a lot of things were a lot more possible than she used to.

"You've been to the hardware store, right?" Jeremiah said.

Robin rolled her eyes and let out an exhausted sigh. "Unfortunately."

"I'm sure you remember Charlie. He's always there and is extremely memorable, especially if you're new here."

"I very clearly remember Charlie. Charlie might have given me trauma."

Jeremiah pointed to a guy at the rear of a group of people. "I think that's him."

Robin could clearly see it. This was definitely the same man they'd run into at the hardware store, but he couldn't have been any older than early twenties. When she'd seen him at the hardware store, she would have thought he was in his early forties at least.

"What are they doing?" Robin said. "Where are they all going?"

"Probably there." Jeremiah pointed to a house that was at least twice as tall as the other tall houses. Robin thought her eyes had adjusted to the darkness and had no idea how she hadn't noticed it before. At the top of the house, only visible at this time of night because of its blinking light, was the longest, thickest lightning rod she'd ever seen.

"What's the plan?" Robin said.

"I don't know what their plan is, but we're going to destroy that house."

"I feel like we should have assembled an army."

"That would have been nearly impossible. Not everyone is loyal to Peter, but almost everyone is too afraid to fight back." He pointed to her knees.

"How has he not gotten to you?"

"Because my family's been here longer than any of these people. And we own our house."

"Yeah. Sure. Piece of cake."

Robin didn't feel good about this at all.

32

WHEN MARCUS LEFT THE GROUP at the fence, he thought about going to go look for Roger, but once he got back onto a main road he didn't see how that would be possible. Now all he wanted to do was get back home. He didn't even care that there was barely a house left. The past couple of nights, he realized he felt more at peace there than he ever had anywhere else. He was excited to see what Peter was going to do with the place. Maybe he'd turn it into a tall house. That would be pretty cool, even though he and Robin didn't really need the space and it'd probably come with a pretty hefty rent increase.

Remembering what he was supposed to be doing, he bellowed "Roger!" into the humid night and, as expected, received absolutely no response. It was weird the way he'd just disappeared like that. He was pretty sure it had something to do with the lightning rods, but that didn't necessarily mean anything bad had happened to him. Maybe the lightning rods were some sort of law enforcement device, there to remove people who were being a problem. Roger wasn't a resident of the village, after all. Maybe the lightning rod just disappeared him from within the village limits and re-appeared him somewhere outside the town. This wasn't at all logical, but it was a tidily wrapped scenario that put his mind at ease, so he decided to accept it.

He needed to get some jars so he could bottle as much of the house's essence he could before it became something else. He was sure there would be a huge demand and, while he wasn't normally one to hang onto his collections, he thought he might have to keep a jar for himself. Robin would probably want one too. He needed to get started on that as soon as possible.

A car with its brights on was coming toward him. For whatever reason, his first instinct was to hide, simply remove himself from the sidewalk and find a lush backyard that would make it hard to find him. But he didn't know why he felt that. Robin had him all worked up. It was her goal to make him afraid of everything.

The car slowed down as it approached him. He recognized the car and found himself getting irrationally excited.

It was Peter.

The car swerved into the opposite lane, pulling alongside Marcus. The windows were already down. Peter leaned across the car, that lunatic grin plastered below those weird eyes, and said, "Get in. We're going rent collecting."

Marcus didn't hesitate. He couldn't get into the car fast enough.

All the seats, except the driver's, had been removed from the car. Marcus couldn't tell if what he was smelling came from the car or from Peter. It smelled like burning oil and ashes. Marcus felt more at ease than he had in a while.

He slammed the door and reached for the seatbelt, which was still there, but there was nothing to plug it into so he left it draped across his chest. Should he tell Peter what Jeremiah and Robin were doing? He didn't think so. It was crazy of them to think Peter had anything to do with this. He was just a landlord. A guy trying to make an honest buck like them. He just happened to be a lot more successful than they were. Marcus had never been the jealous or resentful type and couldn't figure out why Robin had decided to make this all about Peter.

Peter gunned the car and they went flying through town. It was dead. He didn't see a single person on the street. They didn't pass another car the entire ride.

Peter slowed the car and turned onto a gravel drive.

"We gotta guy who just moved in," Peter said in his chipper voice. "Hasn't even paid the deposit yet."

"Wow, yeah," Marcus said. "That's important."

"If I don't collect, I can't keep doing what I'm doing."

"Naturally."

"If I can't keep doing what I'm doing, then nobody gets what they want."

"I understand that."

"I'm glad you were able to come along with me. Because you and Robin are behind. By helping me, you can start chipping away at your wildly spiraling debt."

"We've ... lost some of our revenue streams. We'll think of something eventually."

The headlights shone on a very small, ramshackle house surrounded by towering trees. Peter reached behind his seat and handed a weighty club to Marcus.

"What'm I supposed to do with this?" Marcus said.

"It's the smallest lightning rod I have. It was on the first house I ever built here. Unfortunately it didn't survive its first lightning strike. I'll do all the talking, but sometimes they try to get away. That's when you use the lightning rod."

Marcus held it out in front of him. "Do I just ... *pew-pew!*"

"No. You club them with it. It's a blunt object, not a fucking laser pistol."

"Oh." Marcus brought the rod up and lowered it in a chopping motion.

"That's right," Peter said.

"Definitely has some weight to it."

"Alright. Follow me."

Peter's car door creaked when he opened it. Marcus's also creaked and when he slammed it shut it sounded like a bolt or something came loose from within the car.

He moved closer to Peter and realized the smell from earlier was definitely coming from him and not the car. He followed Peter up onto the rickety porch. Marcus expected him to knock on the door, especially since it was late, but Peter simply turned the knob.

"I need to remember to put something in the lease about locking the doors. I could be anyone and walk right into this house."

The inside of the house was dark until Peter flipped a switch and bathed the living room in light. To Marcus's surprise, Roger was on the floor of the living room. He responded to the light and sluggishly peeled open his bloodshot eyes.

"Where ...?" he mumbled. "Marcus?"

Peter moved quickly. He advanced on Roger while pulling beefy white zip ties from his pocket.

"Roll over on your stomach," Peter said.

"Fuck you, dude," Roger said.

"Club his knees," Peter barked at Marcus.

Marcus reached down and hit one of Roger's knees with the rod.

"Fuck! Why did you do that?" Roger barked.

"We're trying to collect the deposit. It's only fair."

Roger struggled to stand up but couldn't put any weight on his wounded knee. Peter used his leverage to drive him face-first onto the floor and quickly apply the zip ties. Then he hoisted him up and slung him over his shoulder.

"Are we taking him somewhere?" Marcus asked.

"To the founders," Peter said. "They'll be ecstatic."

33

JEREMIAH AND ROBIN WAITED UNTIL the search party was out of sight before crossing the road. They moved as quickly as they could toward the extra tall house. They were halfway there when a flash of lightning lit up the night sky, followed immediately by a boom of thunder that shook the ground and the air around them.

Robin clamped a hand over her mouth to stifle a scream and stopped dead in her tracks. The sudden flash of light had nearly blinded her and the roar of thunder startled her. She wasn't sure where the lightning had landed but she was sure it was the rod on top of the house they were going to burn down. Her body tingled all over and she could feel the tiny blond hairs on her arm stand straight up.

"Come on," Jeremiah hissed at her. "We need to keep—" He stopped short and stared at her, wide-eyed.

"What's wr—"

Robin watched as the hair on Jeremiah's head rose and stood straight out. He looked like a dandelion gone to seed. Robin had visited a science center when she was a kid and remembered how all the other kids had lined up to put their hands on the electro static generator. Their hair stood on end, much like Jeremiah's hair now. She'd been too scared to put her hand on the machine when she was young, afraid it would shock her. She was just as afraid, if not more, now.

"Your hair," he said.

"*Your* hair," she said. She pointed at his head. Tiny zaps sounded and crackles of light flashed around her finger. She pulled her hand back and wrapped her other hand around the finger she pointed at him. "Oh, my god!" she hissed. "Did you see that?"

"We're in an electro static field. We gotta move. Now!"

"What's a elect—"

Jeremiah grabbed Robin's hand and pulled her, trying to get her to run with him. Her fight or flight response kept her cemented where she stood. The air crackled around them. Robin wasn't sure what an electro static field was but she knew she wanted to be as far away from it as possible. She tried to force herself to follow Jeremiah but all her muscles tensed in fear and she felt like a statue.

"Here," he said. He pulled his magic pelt off and flung it over Robin's shoulders. "This will protect you."

Robin thought the pelt smelled heavily of weed and stale beer. A flash of light blinded Robin and she didn't need to be told again to move her ass. The two took off running as the crash of thunder rattled their bones. Robin thought the thunder was going to bust her ear drums. She stumbled as she tried to keep up with Jeremiah.

Jeremiah fumbled in his pocket as they reached the extra tall house. When he pulled his hand from his pocket he dropped something on the sidewalk. The item bounced on the concrete and skittered out into the street.

"Fuck!" he growled.

The item slid to a stop and, in the moonlight, Robin could tell it was a butane lighter.

Jeremiah hadn't taken a full step toward the lighter when a powerful and bright flash of light knocked Robin to the ground. The concrete bit into her forearm. One of her shingle-covered knees made contact with the sidewalk. The earth vibrated beneath her and she covered her ears and squeezed her eyes shut. The thunder blasted through her body. It took her a couple of seconds to realize she *hadn't* been struck by lightning.

Once her senses came back to her, she realized Jeremiah was gone. There was a long, blackened streak on the sidewalk where he'd been standing. The blackened mark splintered and branched out like the root system of a plant and the concrete was smoking.

Robin didn't have time to think of what to do. She jumped up and ran into the street, her knee throbbing. She could feel blood trickling down her leg.

Well, there goes my lucrative career in knee fetish photos, she thought.

She didn't slow down as she bent forward, snapped up the lighter from the middle of the street, and ran in the opposite direction of the extra tall house, afraid of another lightning strike. She needed time to think. She needed to find somewhere she couldn't be seen or wouldn't be killed by lightning. No trees. Nothing metal. And not toward the bonfire and group of people making a racket.

Speaking of …

Everything had fallen quiet. She didn't know why, but the silence scared her more than the deafening thunder.

She dove into a row of hedges dividing the property between two houses. The branches scratched and poked her but she didn't care. She needed to hide. She pulled her knees to her chest and lay as still as possible, trying to catch her breath but also trying to listen for anyone nearby.

Time stretched on forever. It felt like she had been lying in the bushes for at least an hour. She wasn't sure what her plan was. Maybe just lie here until morning and then she could follow someone out the front gates when they went to work.

She needed to move closer to the gate and not be seen. She crawled out of the bushes, trying to make as little sound as possible, and hurried her way into someone's back yard. She hid behind a shed, scuttled to hide behind a tree, and finally ducked behind someone's giant grill. Robin worked her way across Founders' Colony until diving into another thick hedgerow thirty feet from the entrance.

All she had to do now was wait.

Nothing happened and she had no way of telling what time it was or how much time had passed. All she could do was hunker down in the foliage like a carcinoma in situ. As terrified as she was, she was also exhausted. She hadn't done this much cardio in years and certainly had not treated her body like a temple. Robin didn't think it was possible but she almost nodded off.

There was a faint sound and it gave Robin a small adrenaline rush, probably the last of the adrenaline her body could muster. It sounded like an engine in the distance but whatever it was it didn't sound healthy. It revved and slowed, revved and slowed. Robin recognized it as a car. It was getting closer. She peered between two leaves, trying not to disturb the bushes too much and give her location way. She looked at the fence's gate.

Peter's car turned onto the drive of the entrance to Founders' Colony. The moonlight illuminated something strapped to the roof of his car and it was bucking around.

Did he hit a deer? she thought.

She recognized Roger's voice as he yelled for help from the roof of Peter's car. The shadows she was staring at became recognizable in the scant light. Roger was hogtied and strapped to the roof of the car.

34

MARCUS HEARD ROGER SCREAMING AND thrashing
against the roof of the car. Thankfully, in the short ride from Roger's
new home in town, Peter seemed to return to his energetic, positive
mindset. He told Marcus about his car—how it had over two hundred
thousand miles and had never left Little Falls. Peter explained that it
was a stick shift, but he'd never had to leave third gear because there
wasn't a road in town over 25 mph and he liked to obey the laws.

"The speedometer's been broken for the last five years, but I don't
even need it. If I never go higher than third, when the transmission
starts winding, I know I'm going too fast."

This barely made any sense to Marcus, who said, "I never got my
license. I don't know how to drive." He wasn't sure why he lied to
Peter. He just wanted him to stop talking about his car and start talking about his house.

"Then you're not a full man if you don't know the responsibility
of taking care of a vehicle. Taking something mass-produced and
making it your own. Turning it into a utilitarian workhorse that meets

all of your transportation purposes. What I'm saying is that I've turned this car into something magical. It's almost a part of me, at this point."

"Can it, like, fly?"

"No, it doesn't fly ... yet."

Marcus found himself extremely hopeful that it would be able to fly pretty soon.

Peter turned onto a road, the car's headlights illuminating a familiar sight—the gates to Founders' Colony. The brakes squeaked as the car came to a stop and the engine shuddered off with an unhealthy wheezing sound. Marcus thought maybe, wherever Peter came from, the cars were actually living, breathing things.

Peter flipped the headlights on. "Get that asshole off my car," he said.

Marcus got out of the vehicle. He felt terrible. All his muscles ached and his brain swam with confusion. How many times had he been here today alone? He couldn't remember why he'd felt the need to get inside the gates in the first place. He reached up to begin unfastening Roger from the top of the car but was distracted by Peter approaching the entrance.

A figure stood on the other side of the gate. They wore a head-to-toe yellow cloak, the same shade as the lightning bolt shirts. The figure's face was hidden by the hood.

The figure held out its hand. Peter placed his left hand on top of the figure's outstretched one. The figure produced what looked like a really cool knife from its voluminous sleeve. It looked like he sliced one of Peter's fingers and Peter raised his hand so the figure could drink the blood.

Gross, Marcus thought.

The gate magically slid open and Peter stepped to the other side. The cloaked figure disappeared into the shadows inside Founders' Colony. Marcus told himself to remember that all you needed to get in was to donate blood. Seemed so much easier than a ladder and everything the others had had to do.

Marcus *thought* it was Peter who'd stepped inside. There was something odd about him from this distance.

"You haven't even untied him yet. Move your ass!"

Marcus hurriedly unstrapped Roger from the hood of the car. Roger pleaded with him as he worked, and eventually Marcus pulled him off the vehicle. He hit the ground with a thud and a grunt and immediately tried scrambling away. The ties around his ankles and wrists made him look like an uncoordinated worm.

"Drag him to me!" Peter yelled. His voice sounded deeper and more robust than it had when he was in the car.

Marcus clasped the zip-ties binding Roger's wrists and dragged him, screaming, along the drive until he reached the open gate.

"You'll have to wait outside the gate. You can't enter until we transform you."

Marcus had no idea what any of this meant but, being closer to Peter, he was finally able to tell what was different about him.

He was younger.

A lot younger. Marcus imagined this was probably the way Peter looked in college.

"What am I supposed to do?" Marcus said.

"Wait. You know how to do that, don't you?"

Marcus, who felt like he'd spent half his life waiting for things, could absolutely do that.

Peter grabbed Roger's wrist and pulled him inside the gate.

"Fuck you!" Roger barked. He tried to bite Peter's hand but was backhanded.

There was another one of those flashes of light and Peter's eyes darted up toward the sky. Marcus thought he saw something ripple through him. Something electric, or maybe it was just muscle spasms.

"Fuck," Peter said. "I have to go."

Marcus was again confused. Peter crossed the threshold of the open gate and two things happened almost simultaneously. Peter returned to his middle-aged appearance and the gate slammed shut, Roger on the inside, Peter and Marcus on the outside.

"Am I coming with you?" Marcus asked.

"No," Peter said. "This is my white whale. I want to go alone."

"Well …" Marcus threw his hands up. He didn't want to ask what he was supposed to do again because Peter was kind of mean about it last time.

"Keep an eye on that piece of shit." Peter got into his car and quickly backed out onto the road.

With the headlights gone, they were left with scant moonlight. Roger rolled over to face Marcus.

"Help me get out of this, asshole," Roger slurred.

Marcus couldn't tell if he was drunk or if they'd hit him in the head too many times.

"I can't," Marcus said. "Gate's locked."

"Then go get help. Find Jeremiah and Robin."

Marcus thought about leaning against the gate until he remembered that it was electrified. He moved as close to it as he felt comfortable with.

"I think they're in there with you," he said.

"Why are you helping *him*?"

Marcus didn't answer right away. He didn't think anyone had asked him this before. He didn't need to think too long about his answer.

"Because I want a better life for Robin and me."

"It's like making a deal with the devil."

"Oh, we're not religious."

Roger spit at him, rolled away from him, and began shouting for help as loud as he could.

Marcus watched as the shadows of people began to come from the surrounding yards, although Marcus didn't think they were going to help Roger.

It was too dark for Marcus to recognize the first person to approach but they must have been familiar to Roger because he said, "Hey, Rick, can you help me get these fucking things off?"

When Marcus squinted at the guy, he thought he was wearing a Little Falls Brewery t-shirt. Maybe it was one of Roger's co-workers. The guy's stature made him look like he was barely out of his teens. Almost too young to be working at a brewery.

Rick brought back his foot and leveled a vicious kick into Roger's stomach.

"Jesus fucking Christ, Rick," Roger coughed. "What the hell was that for?"

Marcus saw others convene around Roger. He was sure he noticed Charlie from the hardware store, but everyone appeared so young it was hard to tell. There was a person he was sure was wearing a police officer's uniform. Marcus couldn't quite tell if they were a man or a woman and decided it didn't really matter. There were a few other people Marcus thought he recognized from town. None of them paid Marcus any attention.

"Hey, Charlie, give him some of your special seasoning," the cop said.

"Hell, yeah," Charlie said. "I've been waiting for this. I've been eating nothing but peppers for the past week."

Marcus heard the rattle of metal, a zipper, and the splatter of water before it dawned on him they were pissing on Roger.

"Marcus! Go get some fucking help!"

Marcus realized he was watching the violence play out before him with the cool detachment of watching a movie. It occurred to him this was probably not something he should want to watch. Entertaining, sure, and he did think Roger would end up okay, but he understood the optics of it. He slowly backed away from the gate, into the night, knowing Roger would lose sight of him and think he was going to get help.

He wasn't going to get help. He didn't even know where he would begin. He decided to walk around the perimeter of the fence and see if he could see Robin. Maybe he could convince her to come back out and play by the rules. He knew if she just did what they were supposed to do that it was possible for them to end up living in Founders' Colony one day.

Before getting far enough away, Marcus heard Roger shout, "Help!" before unleashing the most blood-curdling scream he'd ever heard.

35

ROBIN SAW WHAT HAPPENED TO Roger. She'd seen the person in the cloak and the exchange with Peter. She stayed rooted in her hiding spot, covered in the goat hide, hoping that Jeremiah was right and that it was magic. She wanted to help Roger, but before she could think of anything to do, the large group of people had already taken him away. At least he was still alive ... for now.

She noticed Marcus wander away—big surprise—and thought maybe she could move to the perimeter of the fence, locate him, and try to talk some sense into him. Maybe she could talk him into somehow helping her get out. The next time Peter showed up Marcus could distract him and she could run through the open gate.

As she slunk back into the shadows, she grew increasingly discouraged. Why had they even bothered doing this? How did they think the four of them were going to be able to take down some evil cabal that ran the town? After all, that's what was happening, wasn't it? The people inside the fence were the same people in town—she recognized a few of them—only younger. If they were all in here for some kind of feast or ritual sacrifice or something, that meant their houses in the village were probably empty right now. She needed to find Marcus and tell him to … to what?

She tried to think.

Kill it with fire.

Maybe he could find a lock somewhere and lock all of them inside. Other than the de-aging, they didn't seem to have any magical powers she'd noticed.

She heard a voice, low in volume but speaking forcefully.

Peter.

She froze. She hadn't heard his car return. How did he get inside?

She glimpsed his shadow, but the person he was talking to was obscured by a shrub.

"What did you tell them?" Peter practically hissed.

"I … I told them we needed to get in there. Why aren't you at their house right now? It should be completely disappeared by this point."

The voice sounded familiar. She crept closer and closer, terrified of snapping a twig or rustling some leaves. The other person came into view. She squinted and what she could see in the darkness shocked her. It didn't sound anything like him. Had it all been an act? Her discouragement grew profoundly.

It was Jeremiah. He was young. Practically a teenager. She would've found it intriguing, like going to a partner's parents' house for the first time and seeing photos of them as a teenager hanging on the wall, if it weren't for the fact that Robin now realized there was something bigger than she could comprehend happening. One thing she did know was she couldn't trust anyone anymore. And she was certain when, or *if* she saw Roger again, he'd also be young … and part of whatever was happening in Little Falls, or in Founders' Colony, or both, was too big for one person to stop.

Robin knew there was no fixing anything anymore. Jeremiah was one of *them*. Roger, if he wasn't one of them, would be soon. And Marcus had drunk the Flavor Aid and was more interested in being Peter's lap dog than her partner. They were all in way too deep. She had to leave town … without them. It was every person for themselves now. All she had to do was hike six miles to the nearest town. But first, she needed to get through Founders' Colony's gate. There had to be another way besides the main road to get out of town. Maybe she could hide out in the woods, wait for the weekend, and stowaway in a tourist's trunk or something.

She'd been shook discovering Jeremiah was a traitor and too in her head to pay much attention to what the two were discussing. Her thoughts were racing, trying to put all the pieces together, and she was exhausted.

"Meow."

The close and sudden sound startled Robin. She jerked, rustling the branches of the bush, and clamped a hand over her mouth to keep from shrieking in fright. Skirt was sticking his head into the foliage, looking at her. That's when she knew it was over for her now too.

The conversation between Peter and Jeremiah came to a quick halt.

"Skirt?" Peter said. He took a few steps toward the cat. "Skirt, buddy, where have you been?"

"Meow."

The cat wiggled its body into the bush and tried to climb into Robin's lap. She was panicking and tried to shove the cat off her but it dug its claws in.

Through the leaves, Robin glimpsed Peter getting closer and, in her head, she was shrieking, FUCK FUCK FUCK FUCK!

"Skirt!" Peter said, sternly. "Get out here now!"

"Meow."

Flight! Robin thought. *Flight! Flight! Flight!*

She grabbed the cat by the scruff and shoved it though the branches roughly.

"*Yyyeooow!*" the cat screeched.

"Skirt!" Peter ran toward the cat.

Robin shoved herself though the bush on the opposite side and took off running.

"There she goes!" Jeremiah shouted. "I told you she was still in here!"

Robin ran faster than she had in her entire life, even though her knee was throbbing. She didn't know where she was going. There was no way out except through or over the fence, which she was sure had been re-electrified. She had to hide again. That was her only option. She would hide and make her way toward the gate when it was safe.

She spotted the dying bonfire in the middle of a street and made a hard left away from it, knowing that was probably where most of the people were.

There was a lot of yelling as she ran blindly through the streets. She didn't have time to sneak her way through the yards in town this time. People were yelling and scurrying around Founders' Colony.

"There! There!" someone yelled.

She risked a glance over her shoulder and spotted a woman a block behind her pointing and shouting. The woman was with a small group of people and they all started running after her. When she refocused on the street in front of her, she realized another group of people was running toward her.

Flight!

She made another hard left, running up the steps of a house, not realizing it was the tallest house in Founders' Colony, the one where lightning had previously terrorized her and disappeared Jeremiah. Robin expected the door to be locked and her backup plan was to reverse defenestrate herself through one of the windows if she had to. She couldn't wrap her head around what the end goal was but all she knew was that she needed to get away from the mob of people chasing her. Roger's screams echoed in her head. To Robin's surprise, the door was unlocked and she barged into the house and ran right into the middle of a large circle of figures in yellow cloaks.

The room was filled with low yellow lighting that danced on the walls. It felt like the house was on fire. Candles sat on every surface in the parlor she'd barged into, including the chandelier suspended from the ceiling.

The group stepped toward her, closing the gaps between them, blocking the door she'd run in through, leaving her nowhere else to run.

Robin lowered into a half crouch, arms out, as if she could take on all the people in the room. She was sweating profusely, panting, and her heart hammered so hard she thought she might actually have a heart attack.

One of the cloaked figures took a step toward her to separate themselves from the others and produced a knife from within their sleeve.

Robin whimpered and took a step back. "Fuck you," she said. "I don—"

The person lifted their free hand to their hood and lowered it.

Robin's brain took seconds to compute what she was seeing. Their skin was pale but pink and spotted brown. The skin was loose and wrinkled, folds of skin drooped over their eyes and made Robin wonder if they could see her or not. But the most disturbing thing was the mouth. Folds of skin opening and closing, pulsing in a perfect circle, like a toothless lamprey. The smell that wafted from the orifice was something Robin could only think of as ancient and evil.

The thing took another step toward her as a bolt of lightning struck the rod on top of the house, shaking the entire structure.

Robin screamed.

36

MARCUS STUMBLED HIS WAY BACK toward town. He was more tired than he thought he'd ever been. He felt lost and direction-less. He didn't know what he was supposed to do. He thought he'd cemented a position as Peter's assistant, but now that seemed up in the air. Maybe he'd just keep walking. He wasn't sure there was any-thing in Little Falls for him. Robin seemed to be so obsessed with battling some opposition that it was taking up all her free time. He couldn't remember which one of them decided to go to war with Pe-ter.

No one was out in town. He imagined they were probably all back at Founders' Colony, having an awesome time. It certainly felt like they were preparing for something there. It somehow made him feel even more left out.

He decided he would head back to the tiny house, grab the few things he needed, and head out of town. He didn't have any money and the only person he could really consider a friend was another jar vendor he'd met online. He'd always told him Marcus was welcome to stay with him if he was ever nearby. The only real problem was that he lived in Australia.

Marcus reached town and noticed all the houses were dark. Not even any security lights were on. No one was in their yards or on their porches. Marcus suddenly found himself growing even more tired than he already was. He wondered if the people of Little Falls locked their doors.

He slowly approached a modest craftsman-style house. Maybe everyone in town was in Founders' Colony. He glanced up at the roof of the house to see a massive lightning rod. He didn't know if the lightning rods symbolized someone was an elite or a renter. Since they had one on theirs, he assumed it meant they were renters.

He took the two steps to reach the porch.

He approached the front door and put his hand on the knob. He was too tired to be nervous. Turning the knob, he wasn't really that surprised to find the door completely unlocked. Little Falls was the type of place where people *usually* felt safe.

Actually stepping into the house was the real surprise. It looked completely abandoned. It was furnished and there were signs of some kind of domestic life occurring here at one time, but everything was covered in a thick layer of dust and looked like it hadn't been used in years. Scanning the first floor, he didn't see anything resembling a bedroom. He was too creeped out by the situation to climb the stairs and look for a proper bed. He just needed to close his eyes.

He went to the plush sofa in the living room and collapsed onto it, sending up a plume of dust. He was too tired to sneeze.

He told himself he would just lie down for a few minutes.

37

SIMPLY BEING IN THE PRESENCE of the thing standing before her stole Robin's will to do absolutely anything. She'd seen plenty of horror movies, sure, but to see something like this in reality, to know on some visceral level it wasn't just a person in a costume, paralyzed her with fear. It was all she could do to look around the large room and try to assess the situation even though it felt like maybe her brain was paralyzed too.

A number of people wearing similar robes were gathered in the large room. She saw other people putting on their robes. They all looked like younger versions of some of the people in town she'd seen before. She saw Charlie from the hardware store. The cop, Penny, who'd been friendly to her. And she imagined all the people whose faces she couldn't see. They were all people who had undoubtedly flashed her a smile and a nod while she was running errands in town.

All the activity gradually drew her gaze to the back of the room. A shrine of some kind took up the entire wall, eerily lit in a shade of piss yellow. There was a symbolic lightning rod statue with a bolt striking it. And in front of the shrine, Roger lay strapped and thrashing to an altar. She was able to force her throat into a gulp when she noticed the two empty altars to his left.

Her brain told her body to run and she attempted to dash away—fast, without even thinking—but her muscles were like jelly and she went spilling onto the floor while the room erupted in laughter. Two robed figures approached her, one of them moving to either side of her. She couldn't see their faces, but she knew this was most likely Peter and Jeremiah.

"You're going to sacrifice us for not paying rent?" she tried to say, but the only thing that came out was a pathetic squeak.

Peter and Jeremiah hoisted her up and began dragging her toward the altar. Whatever fight she'd had was now completely gone. Her body shook with fear and the knowledge that these were possibly her final moments. Her whole life was flashing before her. She wondered how long it would take for anyone she knew to realize she was missing, and thinking about that made her sad she hadn't done more or made more friends during her brief stay on the planet. Now that Marcus was basically one of them, she wondered if he'd even care when she was gone.

Robin didn't even bother to try fighting. She felt like she'd been fighting Peter from day one. This was her conceding the battle to him. Even if she could muster up the energy to run, she knew she wouldn't get very far. And if she got out of the house, she still had to get beyond the fence, and then she'd have to get out of town, which she didn't think she could do without breaking whatever spell had been placed over her or the town.

She couldn't believe she was even thinking like this. Before moving here, she didn't believe in the supernatural. She wasn't and had never even been a religious person.

She felt so powerless she couldn't even muster a scream.

She let herself go completely limp as Jeremiah and Peter lifted her onto the altar and strapped her down.

Only a few months ago, she could have never predicted her life would end like this. She didn't know whether she should remain alert and conscious to try and take everything in or give in to that seductive desire to simply close her eyes and make everything fade to black in a traumatic haze.

The monstrous figure in the hood she'd seen before stood at the feet of the altars. It raised its head to shout at the room of people.

"Bring me the third!"

Suddenly, the room was a chaotic scramble as people practically tripped over themselves to leave the room and go searching for Marcus.

38

MARCUS AWOKE ONLY A FEW minutes after falling asleep to a loud boom of thunder and a bright flash of lightning. He felt oddly refreshed and less panicked. He guessed he should probably get out of this house and go look for Peter. He got up from the sofa and walked to the front door. Opening the door, he second-guessed himself and thought maybe he should just hang out in the house for a few more minutes. Rain lashed the side of the house. The thunder and lightning were nearly constant.

Where the hell did this come from? he wondered. But he didn't think about it too much. He couldn't remember the last time he'd looked at his phone or the TV. The weather people could have been calling for the storm of the century for all he knew.

He didn't want to go back into the house. He felt an amazing sense of purpose. He felt like tonight was the night something was going to happen. Tonight was surely the night they'd be welcomed into the inner fold.

He stepped off the porch and into the raw elements.

He was promptly struck by lightning.

He may have lost consciousness for a moment or two as he lay next to the road with the rain beating down on him.

Opening his eyes, he could smell something charred and figured that was probably him.

He felt oddly calm. He took a deep breath.

The lightning made him think about jars for some reason. What was that old expression? "Like lightning in a jar." No. That wasn't quite right. "Lightning in a bottle." That was it. Bottle. Jar. Same thing. He wondered if he could capture lightning in a jar.

He hopped up, his soaked clothes sagging around him.

He hadn't been this inspired in a while. It was almost like he could feel the lightning surging through him.

Mentally, he made a change of plans. Something was going on in Founders' Colony, for sure. But right now, he had better things to do. He'd always prioritized creativity over everything else and knew if he didn't act now, he might lose the opportunity. He was sure there would always be another ritual, but when a creative impulse is gone, it's gone for good. Or at least that had always been the case with him.

He put Peter and Robin and the whole town of Little Falls out of mind.

He needed to get to the hardware store.

Thankfully, everything in town was only a few blocks away. The rain and wind thrashed him and he wondered if he'd get struck by lightning again. Not that he would really mind. He hadn't felt this clear-headed in a while.

When he got to the hardware store, he didn't even bother trying the door to see if it was locked. He picked up a large rock from a flowerbed nearby and threw it through the glass. The crash was satisfying. He stepped into the musty store and his eyes went directly to the gleaming wall of jars. He looked at the few jars on the counter— Charlie's attempt to compete with him—and shook his head. "Garage." "Bedroom." "Sunny day." He was a complete novice. The jarred essence market was niche. People wanted to be reminded of things they didn't think about all the time. No one wanted the essence of a garage unless something truly wild and magical was happening in it.

Marcus took a quick lap of the store and found a Radio Flyer wagon. It was mostly metal, so he didn't know if it would be great in the lightning, but he didn't really care. The important thing was that he load up on jars and get back out there so he could try to capture it. He took the wagon down from its hook in the wall and began loading it with jars, unscrewing the lids as he did so. He found a small jar, about the size of a baby food jar, and didn't know if it was big enough to do anything but added it anyway.

It wasn't long before the wagon was loaded and he was wheeling it outside the store.

The lightning hadn't stopped. If anything, it had intensified, dancing across the sky like neon veins. Maybe that was the real reason for all the lightning rods—to try and attract the lightning to Little Falls. Maybe it was essential to all the weirdness happening here. Or maybe Little Falls was a lightning hotspot and Peter was trying to harvest its raw power.

With his newfound clarity, Marcus marched through the angry weather on his way to Founders' Colony. He realized Robin was right. They needed to get the fuck out of here. He felt ashamed of himself for not having tried much sooner. They should have left after the first bit of weirdness. He should've trusted Robin's instincts. Peter creeped her out right away. He didn't know how he'd ever been convinced Peter had their best interests at heart. No one with any amount of empathy ever becomes a landlord. A landlord is a person who looks at people as consumers and their well-being as a product that has to be paid for.

He reached the gates of Founders' Colony, not that surprised to not see anyone outside in the storm. The jars were filled with a little bit of rainwater and, he hoped, lightning. He screwed the lids on and hoped for the best. He pulled one of the jars from the wagon and hurled it at the gate.

39

ROBIN HAD SHUT DOWN MENTALLY. She retreated into herself, into a thoughtless void. It was all too much for her. The mind can only take so much before it overloads and needs to reset. She wasn't sure how long she had dissociated before a crash of lightning brought her to her senses. She kept her eyes shut, hoping anyone in the room would think she was still out of it.

Rain pelted the house and there were constant booms of thunder. Roger whimpered nearby. With her eyes shut, Robin couldn't be sure if there was anyone else in the room. There was no rustle of robes or voices. She chanced a peek and spotted the creature in the middle of the room, unmoving, watching them. Everyone else had either left or retreated to other rooms in the house.

Robin didn't feel like she had much left to lose. She was certain these were the last few minutes of her life and it just didn't feel fair or make any sense. What had she done in her life to deserve this? She definitely hadn't lived the most conservative life, but she also wasn't a monster. Was it too much to ask to be happy, and to share that happiness with a partner, and to make enough money to scrape by, and to enjoy what you did to make a living, and to have a roof over your head each night? Why was she being punished? Why was she about to die?

"Why are you doing this?" Robin opened her eyes and stared at the creature in the middle of the room.

Seconds passed and the figure did not answer. Robin thought about asking again but she knew they'd heard her the first time. There was no use in wasting energy trying to figure out why she was about to be murdered. She wasn't going to repeat herself.

Suddenly, there was a boom, accompanied by a blinding blue light that filled all the windows of the house. The blue light only lasted a few seconds, then the house was filled with stillness. At least the candles were still lit and she thought she saw a look of slight concern on the figure's face still staring at her.

40

THE WET JAR SLIPPED FROM Marcus's hand as he tried to throw it at the fence. At first, he thought the jar was going to miss the fence altogether, but the jar spiraled straight toward a black electrical box attached to the fence by the gate. When the jar hit the box the world was filled with a blinding blue light and sparks and horrendous electrical booming zaps.

Marcus threw his arm up to cover his eyes and the explosion knocked him off his feet. He thought the bright light had permanently blinded him, but then lightning flashed and made silhouettes of the world. It took him a few seconds to get his bearings. Lightning flashed a few more times and he could see the shadows of the houses in Founders' Colony.

The only source of light was the random flashes from the storm. It was difficult to see anything except when the lightning lit up the sky and Marcus was forced to wait on nature's strobe light to see. He approached the gate, reluctantly reached out to touch it, and was relieved when it didn't shock him. Marcus pulled on the gate door and it opened.

He was in.

Marcus contemplated taking the wagon with him but figured it was too much work to pull it along. Besides, he didn't think he really had a need for it any more. He grabbed the small baby food jar and put it in the pocket of his shorts. It comforted him to keep at least one jar on him.

He had no idea where he needed to go and started wandering the streets of Founders' Colony, lit sporadically by the lightning. The rain was falling so hard the streets were beginning to flood. A massive bolt of lightning hit a lightning rod on top of what Marcus thought might be the largest house in the addition. The house was a little over a block away, and when the light faded, he noticed a soft yellow glow in the windows of the first floor. He looked at the houses around him and didn't see any other windows lit up.

"There he is!"

Marcus looked down the street to his right. When the light in the sky flashed, he spotted a group of four people in yellow robes with flashlights, one of them pointing directly at him. They all stared at him for a beat before they took off running toward him.

The group's enthusiasm renewed his desire to stay in Little Falls and be a part of something larger than himself. Marcus raised his hand and waved it above his head. "I'm over here, guys!"

Marcus was so excited to finally become part of their group. It looked like they'd been waiting for him to come back so they could welcome him into the fold. He was so happy and couldn't wait to hang out with Peter again. He was certain he could be Peter's helper when it came to collecting rent and he wanted to erase his debt with Peter. Also, he was hoping that once he became part of the group they'd give him one of the houses in Founders' Colony. He wanted one of those yellow robes and it would be really nice to change out of his soaked clothes.

The group ran full-speed at him and he kept waving. Before he knew it, the group had tackled him to the ground.

"Stop fighting!" one of the cloaked figures screamed.

Marcus lay on the ground. "I'm fine. I'm okay, guys."

"Stop resisting!" another yelled.

A third one kicked him in the stomach, knocking the wind out of him. Another kicked him in the head. Someone hit him on the head with their flashlight.

"Ouch!" Marcus curled into a ball in the flooded street. "You're hurting me! Stop! I'm one of you!"

"Stop resisting!"

"I'm not!"

"Grab him!"

Each of the figures grabbed one of Marcus's limbs and started dragging him down the street, headed toward the house with the glowing windows. Marcus was glad because the house looked like the place to be.

41

ROBIN COULD HEAR THE FOUNDERS' Colony residents storming back into the house. She glanced back at the figure in front of her, wondering if her eyes were playing tricks or if the figure had somehow multiplied, because there were now three figures standing in front of her. The sight of their shriveled, almost desiccated skin made her thankful for the low lighting.

Along with the footsteps of the returning residents, she heard another sound she found all too familiar.

Marcus's high-pitched shrieking.

And she found herself no longer wistful for the future but nostalgic for the past. Whatever had happened to him, Peter was to blame. This was what she told herself. She would do anything just to go back to that halcyon moment where they were happy enough in their downtown apartment but elated about continuing their life in a place like Little Falls.

Even with everything happening around her, she couldn't help critiquing Marcus's and her choices. They should have taken a more affordable apartment. Or did what her parents wanted her to do and rent a house closer to them. You know, just in case they wanted to have kids, even though she was a little long in the tooth to be having children. Her mom even offered to help pay for it.

She felt so dumb.

And it felt like she was getting dumber by the second.

It felt like her brain was melting because what was happening around her really shouldn't be happening. It shouldn't even be possible in the physical world she grew up in and thought she knew so well.

She was strapped to an altar with Marcus's blacked-out brother on another altar to her left and an empty altar presumably for Marcus to her right while three creatures that looked barely human slobbered and oozed in front of her. She was in a house she hadn't even known existed until a little while ago and this all seemed to be the center of some ceremonial ritual. The yellow-robed figures had now flooded back into the room and there was an air of anticipation.

Hell, at this point, she found herself a little curious too.

What was going to happen?

She assumed it wasn't going to be great for her and Marcus and Roger. A metaphor for life, she guessed. Everything they had worked so hard for would just be absorbed by these incredibly wealthy individuals around them.

Two of the robed figures brought Marcus in front of the creatures at the foot of the altars. One of them licked its lips with a rotten-looking tongue.

Marcus turned to look at Robin.

She didn't recognize him in that gaze. He was either completely gone or completely traumatized.

Robin screamed.

42

WHEN MARCUS LOOKED INTO ROBIN'S eyes, he was confused. He didn't see the same hope and wonder he felt. She issued a long scream that got everyone in the room's attention, but it didn't really serve any purpose.

"You'll see," he said. "This is going to be the best thing that's ever happened to us."

As if on cue, Peter and Jeremiah entered the cavernous room. All the robed figures that weren't keeping a tight grip on Marcus fell to their knees and shouted, "Lightning!"

Marcus shouted "lightning" too but he was a little late and it made him feel awkward and crazy. He resentfully looked at Jeremiah and wondered why that wasn't him.

Peter was in his Founders' Colony mode. He looked young and super fit, his formerly thin hair now a flowing river of blond. It looked like lightning itself danced behind his blue eyes.

Peter spread his arms out to his sides, looking amazingly Christlike.

"You have all done an amazing job. I'm glad you realize the benefits you receive from being my followers. Eternal youth. Fantastic real estate. A sense of true purpose."

Another round of communal "Lightning!" This time Marcus was on it. It must be their version of "Amen."

Peter continued: "And to keep all those benefits, we all understand that sacrifices have to be made. Everyone outside these gates sees me as a landlord. And I think I'm probably the greatest landlord ever."

"Lightning!"

Peter beamed. He'd always seemed pretty upbeat but now he seemed completely radiant. Marcus thought he might have even been emitting a bluish glow.

"But within these gates, you all know me as the bodylord. The living spaces I'm expected to maintain on the outside are no different than the bodies I must preserve on the inside. I spend my time on the outside looking for the perfect occupants to act as stewards to my properties. But what's really important is how they serve us here, on the inside. This is our heaven—an evolving, eternal paradise!"

"Lightning!"

Peter motioned to the three creatures at the foot of the altar. This was the first time Marcus noticed them. They didn't look human. More like yellowish piles of rotting meat.

"When I notice people here are sick and aging, it is my job to find replacement vessels for them. And that is why we are here tonight. I have not let you down. When the body is in need of nourishment, I am the one who will plant and harvest the fruit. And tonight is the night we partake of that fruit. So these three followers will know what it's like to feel young and beautiful and strong again."

"Lightning!"

"And by accepting my offer of these three hosts, they commit to a life within the colony, making it even better for everyone."

"Lightning!"

Marcus shouted along with everyone else but wondered exactly what Peter meant. Maybe they'd share their bodies with these creatures. Marcus wasn't sure if he wanted to share his body with another person. Something about it felt invasive. He wanted to ask Peter some questions but this didn't seem to be the Q-and-A portion of the speech or sermon or whatever it was.

"Unfasten the gifts and ready them for transference."

"Lightning! Lightning!"

The room was suddenly swirling with motion. The hands of the robed figures surrounding Marcus began removing his clothes. He couldn't remember the last time he'd taken a shower. He looked toward the altars to see a mass of robed figures unshackling Roger and Robin. Marcus's t-shirt was ripped off and fingers were working the button of his shorts. Material got snagged on the pieces of the tiny house attached to his arms. The people yanked on the clothing, causing Marcus pain as the act nearly ripped the pieces of house from his body.

He watched them rip Roger's loose clothes off. Marcus hadn't seen Roger naked since they were kids. Marcus didn't realize he was that hairy. He also didn't realize Roger had so many tattoos.

When he glanced at Robin, she was already naked except for the shingles covering her knees. Two robed figures worked at removing them. Marcus realized he was now also fully naked except for the planks of wood on him, which they were also in the process of removing.

Marcus glanced back at Robin because he was curious to see her knees after so long.

There they were.

He remembered this was actually his first introduction to Robin. He never had money to tip her Bee's Knees page, but he managed to find her on that entrepreneurial forum and they'd had some meaningful exchanges.

They really were great knees. It was almost like they had some sort of power over him.

The robed figures pulled Marcus over to Robin and Roger. Roger, who was still unconscious, had to be supported by two of the figures. Marcus moved close enough for his arm to touch Robin's.

She leaned her head close to him and said, "Come back to me."

43

ONLY A FEW MOMENTS BEFORE, Robin had felt close to having an out-of-body experience. If this was happening, she wanted to be able to dissociate completely, lose herself in memories of better times, to remember life as something good and not the miserable hellscape it had ultimately become. She didn't believe in any sort of afterlife, at least not anything she would be conscious or aware of, so she guessed this was it. She had hoped to die peacefully in her sleep as a very old woman but she guessed giving her body up to a rich old property owner was at least … interesting? How many people did that really happen to? Or at least how many people did that happen to outside of Little Falls? If she had access to make a livestream, she was sure she'd get record amounts of views.

She'd told Marcus to come back to her but he seemed to be going through something. She hoped he wasn't completely lost. He kept staring at the pile of clothes they'd made between them and the three creatures and moving his mouth without making any sounds. Mentally, though, she was still shutting down, preparing for the end. She couldn't waste any of her precious end-of-life energy wondering what was going through Marcus's brain.

Peter moved in front of them, straddling the pile of clothes.

He raised each of his muscular arms toward the sky.

"And now, I will summon the lightning from the heavens. It will light up every lightning rod in town and we'll all feel the charge, the energy."

"Lightning!"

Robin cringed when she realized that was what Marcus was trying to say.

"Let it flow over you! Let it flow through you! Now let's form the circle of power!"

"Lightning!"

The robed figures formed a circle around Marcus, Robin, Roger, and the three creatures. The figures restraining them had to let go to join the circle.

Roger promptly fell to the ground in an unconscious heap.

Marcus stood dazed.

Robin had the immediate desire to bolt. She didn't know if she'd ever actually been physically restrained other than a few times she'd explored a certain sexual kink. It was freeing to feel that go away, but she knew if she tried to escape, she wouldn't make it. They were far outnumbered and overpowered.

Standing there, she had an amazing moment of clarity. While she had seen some things since moving to Little Falls she couldn't explain, it suddenly occurred to her that what Peter was talking about was complete and total horseshit. This transference business was nonsense. The impending new reality, while not death, would be something much worse. Of course the souls of these creatures wouldn't take over her, Marcus's, and Roger's bodies. They would only act like they did. That's what any religion is—the belief in something that isn't real. It's self-gaslighting. It's how they get people to stay in the cult. They would still exist, there just wouldn't be anybody around them who would acknowledge their existence.

Now Peter raised both arms above his head and pressed his palms together, trying to make himself into a human lightning rod.

"It is time to summon the power from the heavens to restore these three to their rightful, youthful vessels."

Everyone shouted "Lightning!" and she could finally hear Marcus muttering.

"Lightning in a bottle. Lightning in a bottle."

And then he flung himself toward the pile of clothes.

Because of the current rapturous state of Peter and his followers, Marcus was probably given a couple seconds he wouldn't have had if anyone was still paying attention to them.

He dropped to his knees before Jeremiah shot out of the pack like an attack dog and landed on his back.

Many of the followers were still standing with their hands locked in a circle, repeatedly shouting "Lightning! Lightning!"

Marcus got his hands on his pair of shorts and ripped them off the pile of clothes. Jeremiah grabbed his arm and Marcus dropped the shorts. They made a loud thump and what looked like a small, empty jar came rolling out. Before she could be re-restrained, Robin reached for it.

With Jeremiah still on his back, Marcus shouted, "Throw it!"

Robin didn't see what throwing an empty jar would do.

Peter, his head still very far up his own ass, continued to stand with his palms pressed together over his head.

Robin figured an empty jar was probably only good as a weapon, something to be hurled at someone.

She looked at Peter and thought about how much she'd wanted to do this ever since the first time he'd creeped them out. She moved behind Roger to provide at least some kind of barrier between her and the followers. She brought the jar back in her hand and trained her sight on Peter's beatific face.

She threw it with everything she had, which admittedly was not very much.

It struck him in the chin, the sound of it shattering suddenly the loudest thing in the room.

44

JEREMIAH'S FISTS WERE NOT LARGE, but they were very painful every time they struck the back of Marcus's head. He was unable to pay attention to Robin, but he was still thinking about her knees. He hoped she got her hands on the jar, but he was willing to accept whatever was happening to him. He figured it would be kind of like living in a duplex. He'd have to share the building with someone else but neither one of them would own it. He guessed Peter would kind of own it. And they wouldn't be able to leave the Colony. If he'd understood that correctly. But in the brief time they'd been here, it seemed like a fine place, and he was sure people from the outside could bring him anything he needed.

Then he heard the sound of shattering glass and the whole place lit up with a blinding blue glow, electricity crackling the air. He didn't know if this was his lightning or the energy transferred here by hundreds of lightning rods. He closed his eyes and waited to see if he could feel someone else move into his body.

Thankfully, Jeremiah's hands stopped hammering the back of his head and he felt almost calm. Maybe this was how it had to happen. Maybe the body had to shut down, everything relaxing to make the new environment more pliable for the new occupants.

He kept his head down, basking in the lingering blue light.

45

WHAT WAS HAPPENING WAS THE closest thing to miraculous she'd ever seen.

Peter, his chin bloodied, dropped to his knees and belted out a howl of rage. Robin watched as he reverted back to his normal form. Somehow he seemed to be even older and slightly decrepit. She watched as the creatures in front of her became more human. They looked surprised. Like their sacrifice dynamic, it was two men and a woman. By the small opening in their yellow robes she could tell they were naked and Robin thought they were maybe middle-age, probably ten years older than Marcus and her. Like her, they turned to survey the chaos in the room.

The robed figures, many of whom had already either lowered their hoods or removed their robes altogether, were all descending on Peter.

They no longer looked young and beautiful. Whatever had happened when Robin struck Peter with the jar seemed to have broken some sort of spell.

Some of the people were young, but for the most part, they resembled any cross-section of a slightly affluent Midwest town.

Jeremiah was still trying to defend his leader.

Robin had thought he seemed so confident and assured, but now she saw him as a relatively small man who was currently drunk and high out of his mind. Whatever mass hysteria had been broken did not affect Jeremiah. She imagined the reality surrounding him was not the same reality as everyone else. Had Peter made him this way? How much sympathy for him should she really have?

"Is the fire still going?" She recognized Charlie from the hardware store. Not the young godlike Charlie she'd witnessed earlier this evening. It was just the slightly malnourished, unwashed Charlie she'd seen at the hardware store/comedy club/concert venue.

Peter leapt to his feet and took a defensive stance. He held his palms out to them like his hands could shoot lightning.

"We have to believe! We have to have faith!" he shouted.

But they had already circled around him and there were far too many of them to stop.

The followers now smothered Peter and Jeremiah and lifted them above their heads.

"With all the rain, I don't see how the fire could still be going," Penny said.

"We have to have faith," Mattie responded.

They both laughed at that.

They began marching Peter and Jeremiah toward the front of the cavernous room.

Robin walked over to Marcus and nudged his side with her foot. She picked her clothes out of the pile and said, "You might want to come and watch this."

46

MARCUS ROLLED OVER AND LOOKED at Robin. She was pulling her clothes on and her knees were the first thing he saw. He glanced over his shoulder and saw the followers leaving the room with Peter and Jeremiah held over their heads.

He sat up.

"Where are they going?" he said to Robin.

"I think they're going to throw Peter and Jeremiah into the fire."

Marcus fell silent.

"Does that mean ...?" he finally asked.

"I think it's over."

He stood up, not feeling as battered as he thought he would, and picked his clothes out of the heap.

He asked, "Should we wake Roger up?"

"I don't think we should disturb him. He's on his stomach. He'll be okay."

Marcus hurriedly put on his clothes and followed Robin outside. Looking back at the house, he was disappointed to see that it wasn't nearly skyscraper height. It was practically a shack. Even more of a shack than the tiny house they'd moved into that he could barely remember. He realized it was the shack from the woods. The one he thought they'd burned down. Maybe they'd just moved it. He didn't really know. He couldn't really remember much of anything since that night.

Somehow, as impossible as it seemed, the fire was now raging, but there was something ominous in the air. The rain had stopped but lightning still flashed in the distance, the storm now a fading dream. Looking at the night sky was like looking at one of those plasma lamps. It looked like all the lightning rods were communicating, sending out swirling tendrils of electricity that lit up the night sky.

They pulled up behind the group of followers. No one else seemed too concerned about what was going on overhead.

"Save us, lightning rods!" Peter shouted, still defiant, hands still raised in the air.

Marcus and Robin surrounded the fire with the followers.

In what was apparently a last-minute crisis of faith, Peter and Jeremiah both began shouting "I'm sorry! I'm sorry! I'm so sorry!"

The collective strength of the followers was enough to launch them both into the air before they dropped into the center of the raging fire.

It devoured them hungrily. Their screams died almost as quickly as they'd started. The townspeople watched in silence as the two in the fire stopped moving and the fire melted and ate their flesh.

The electricity disappeared from the sky and, through the clouds, they all watched as the deep shade of purple dawn emerged. A mourning dove cooed its first song of the day in a nearby tree.

One by one, the group of people broke apart and started walking toward the open gate of Founders' Colony.

Robin took Marcus's hand in hers and said, "Let's go home."

ANDERSEN PRUNTY is the author of several novels, novellas, and short stories. He lives in Yellow Springs, Ohio. Visit him online at notandersenprunty.com.

C.V. HUNT is a co-writer of this book, among other things. Visit their site at cv-hunt.com.

Other Grindhouse Press Titles

#666__*Satanic Summer* by Andersen Prunty

#112__*The Freakshow: Rebirth in Drayton Falls, Volume 2* by Bryan Smith

#111__*Drive-Thru of the Dead: Drayton Falls, Volume 1* by Bryan Smith

#110__*Inhospitable* by Ali Seay

#109__*Violência* by Sultan Z. White

#108__*From the Void* by Bryan Smith

#107__*Corpse Mountain* by Andersen Prunty

#106__*Depraved Halloween* by Bryan Smith

#105__*Dread Ink* by Bryan Smith

#104__*Jack and Mr. Grin* by Andersen Prunty

#103__*What Ever Happened to Jo Rose?* by Chris DiLeo

#102__*I Think I'm Alone Now* by Ali Seay

#101__*Cute Aggression* by Emily Lynn

#100__*Headless* by Scott Cole

#099__*The Killing Kind* by Bryan Smith

#098__*An Affinity for Formaldehyde* by Chloe Spencer

#097__*Kill The Hunter* by Bryan Smith

#096__*The Gauntlet* by Bryan Smith

#095__*Bad Movie Night* by Patrick Lacey

#094__*Hysteria: Lolly & Lady Vanity* by Ali Seay

#093__*The Prettiest Girl in the Grave* by Kristopher Triana

#092__*Dead End House* by Bryan Smith

#091__*Graffiti Tombs* by Matt Serafini

#090__*The Hands of Onan* by Chris DiLeo

#089__*Burning Down the Night* by Bryan Smith

#088__*Kill Hill Carnage* by Tim Meyer

#087__*Meat Photo* by C.V. Hunt and Andersen Prunty

#086__*Dreaditation* by Andersen Prunty

#085__*The Unseen II* by Bryan Smith

#084__*Waif* by Samantha Kolesnik

#083__*Racing with the Devil* by Bryan Smith

#082__*Bodies Wrapped in Plastic and Other Items of Interest* by Andersen Prunty

#081__*The Next Time You See Me I'll Probably Be Dead* by C.V. Hunt